FREE CITY

A RED BRANCH MISSION
BOOK 4

BLAZE WARD

KNOTTED ROAD PRESS

Free City
A Red Branch Mission: 4
Blaze Ward
Copyright © 2025 Blaze Ward
All rights reserved
Published by Knotted Road Press
www.KnottedRoadPress.com

ISBN: 978-1-64470-465-3

Cover Art: GetCovers.com

Cover and interior design copyright © 2025 Knotted Road Press

Reviews
It's true. Reviews help. Even a short one, such as, "Loved it!" So please consider reviewing this book (and all of the ones you've read) on your favorite retailer site.

Never miss a release!
If you'd like to be notified of new releases, sign up for my newsletter.

http://www.blazeward.com/newsletter/

Buy More!
Did you know that you can buy directly from the Knotted Road Press website?

https://www.knottedroadpress.com/shop/

The Hunter Bureau

Start with: Mirrors

Fairchild

Start with: Fairchild

Last Stand

Start with: Lost Dreams

The Lazarus Alliance

Start with: Escape

Shadow of the Dominion

Start with: Longshot Hypothesis

Star Dragon

Start with: Birth of the Star Dragon

Kincaide's War

Start with: The Eden Package

Star Tribes

Start with: Winterstar

Blaze also writes Action-Adventure Here

CONTENTS

ESSAY: THE FREE CITY

When I started planning for book four in the Red Branch, I knew my era was early in 1950, but I absolutely didn't want to set any part of the story during the Korean War. Soviet mercenaries would not be welcome there, and it was the US Navy that held the line in those early months, because Air Force jets based in Japan had just enough range to get there, spend about five minutes, then race home.

It was only after squadrons could be moved to the peninsula that USAF got deeply involved, so early navy jets fought MiG-15s. And got their asses handed to them, because the only thing we really had that was the 15's peer was the F-86 Sabre. And then only barely, because it was the later D-variant that really earned the legend.

Early on, the Americans were flying B-29 and B-50 (the upgraded 29 with improvements) and trying to day-bomb targets. They got slaughtered by MiGs, so ended up shifting to nighttime operations.

As has been noted in previous books by a number of characters, there was something of a revolution in jet aviation every year from at least 1944 to about 1956, when the Brits decided to blow up their entire research capability, instead going all in on nuclear weapons and missiles to deliver them. Khrushchev did much the same thing when he eventually took supreme power after Stalin died and everyone agreed to shoot Beria like the mad dog sex fiend that he was.

A lot of money will be poured into nukes and missiles, but that's the latter portion of the 1950s, outside our current scope. (And no, I have no idea at what point I will run out of ideas for the Red Branch. As I write this, I'm in the middle of editing #5 while plotting #6 and realizing that I have notes for what might be 7 & 8. Lots to do, and little of it will be Korea or French Indochina.)

In 1950, you have only a few countries building capable combat jets, though many are madly trying to keep up. The Swede have always kept their own council and built the Saab 21R (adapted from the piston-driven 21) and the Saab 29 Tunnan (aka The Flying Barrel). The Americans and the Brits built the best kit, but the Soviets introduced the MiG-15 and bottled lightning with that design, something so excellent that only the F-86 Sabre was a match.

American pilots tended to be better trained than their Soviet (flying North Korean jets) counterparts, so they could compete with slower aircraft. And did, in straightwing piston-driven aircraft like the North American F-51D Mustang or the North American F-82F/G Twin Mustang. The Lockheed F-80C Shooting Star could duel with a MiG-15, but not well, just like the Republic F-84D/E Thunderjet and Lockheed F-94B Starfire were too slow.

It took the Sabre to win supremacy the air. And they did.

But again, I didn't want to be in that war, because too

many people know too much about it and will nit-pick every detail I might get wrong. And I'm sure I would. Nature of fiction, where fun needs to sometimes outmaneuver technical.

At the same time, I've been on a research kick. Learning a lot of South American history that never got taught to Anglos in Norte Americano schools (go figure). Here, I wanted to explore the burgeoning Cold War.

East versus West, but Tito basically told Stalin to go piss up a rope. Digging in, I came to realize that a lot of folks disagreed with the second Communist Emperor of Russia, but weren't in a position to do anything about it. Ask Trotsky. Mexico. 1940.

Tito went neutral. Wanted to actually follow Marxism (the horrors) instead of Stalinism (which had almost nothing in common) and work on the withering of the state. Pushing power down to factory soviets instead of centralizing the entire economy at the capital in a single office, like Stalin and his flunkies had done. Did. Were doing.

As I researched, what I found was that Tito was an early proponent and participant (with a lot of others) in what would become the Third World/Non-Aligned movement. Folks who didn't want to get sucked into Soviet-backed communism/tyranny any more than they wanted Imperial Capitalism in the form of Great Britain or the United States. I haven't come forward past the reunion in '53 after Stalin dies to see how seriously Tito pursued it, but I know that Yugoslavia was always something of a twilight zone, even in the 1980s when I was a kid and the Wichita State University had *Slovenian* Zarko Durisic and *Serbian* Zoran Radović playing on some power-house NCAA basketball teams.

And all the things you'll see about the Yugoslav Air Force

defecting back to the Soviet Union when Tito went neutral really happened. That was where I wanted to have a little fun. *Centre* (the Soviet equivalent of the CIA from so many bad movies) really was like that. I've done too much research on those various organizations.

But what if the UN could broker a deal whereby ex-Soviet mercenary pilots, flying modern American-built jets, could patrol the skies of Yugoslavia while everyone kind of kept quiet and negotiated deals to figure out what might happen next?

And, better, Trieste came THAT CLOSE to ending up as another Monaco on Italy's eastern frontier. Except that Tito wanted to claim it and spall off big chunks of Austria, while Stalin refused to allow any civilian governor to take office under the power-sharing agreements. Eventually, it returns to Italian control, but there's a huge "What if...?" moment to be had there, and that's half the fun.

And I wanted a whole second thread to the story, because each of the first five Red Branch books follow one of the principals: Yuri, Lyuba, Gennadi, Vanya, Yuri.

Vanya's turn.

The man was a NKVD assassin and other things before the war. Then a commissar and pilot. Man of many talents, originally hired by Gennadi to provide the calm, cool, Spock to Sasha's Kirk, if you will.

But what's under that cold, rigid exterior? Who is the man himself, because none of the Red Branch have really gotten to know him. Arkadi is his partner on sniper missions, but that's marked by long periods of dead silence where you communicate by smell and telepathy more than words.

Trieste, then, becomes a boiling pot of trouble, with Yugoslav partisans just over the border. Soviet spies and assassins hiding in plain sight.

And Soviet-trained air forces just over each border, all set to swoop in and commit air piracy and night strikes against Tito's people and the Red Branch.

And that's when things get messy.

When Vanya's past walks in the door.

AIRCRAFT RESEARCH: TRANSITION

A lot of piston-driven aircraft were built just before and during World War 2. The state of the art jumped ahead by tremendous leaps, time and again, especially when you consider that some of the people in charge had been born before powered aircraft.

Kitty Hawk and the Wright Brothers date to December 17, 1903, after all. World War 1 featured cloth over wooden frames on biplanes. It was only in the 1930s that you get all-metal construction. Monoplane shapes. All the famous technology that becomes the Second War.

Jet engines actually predate the war, but nobody had sorted things out properly. The Brits had their Gloster Meteor in service as of July 1944 and the de Havilland Vampire doesn't get introduced until 1946. The Lockheed P-80 was just about to enter service in 1945 when the war ended. The Germans had the Messerschmitt Me 262 from April 1944 and the Heinkel He 162 Volksjäger from January 1945, but not in big enough numbers to matter, regardless of how exceptional they were as individual aircraft.

Everyone basically flew piston-driven aircraft. Fought the war with them, the Allies eventually forming enormous bomber formations to level Germany and Japan while be escorted by fantastic aircraft like the P-51 Mustang or the P-38 Lightning.

They won on an economic footing, because if your factories stop working, you stop producing the part needed to maintain a modern military.

Five years later in 1950, you are now seven years—seven REVOLUTIONS—into the jet age. And the F-90B Strix was designed to be an All-everything fighter-bomber that was as fast as any American aircraft flying. The MiG-15 was generally incapable of reaching Mach 1 and surviving. American and British Cold War bomber tactics were designed originally around the concept of flying higher and faster than any Soviet defensive fighter could stop you. Worked for most of the 1950s, until better jets and better Surface-To-Air Missiles (SAM) were available to shoot down intruding American nuclear bombers.

That was part of the reason to jump to ICBMs, for both sides.

But we're only in 1950, and most of the now-Soviet-dominated nations of what would become the Warsaw Pact in a few years were stuck with old surplus from World War 2. Even new stuff was badly outdated, and a lot of it got sold to South American and newly-independent Asian nations as second-hand gear.

Put simply, nothing that fought in World War Two in the air could hold its own against a modern jet like the F-86, the MiG-15, or the F-90B Strix. I had a lot of fun digging in to see what Albania and Romania were actually flying in that era. Crap.

The Soviet Union, of course had the MiG-15, but wasn't sharing it with folks that might have only joined the cause recently. (Romania was a Nazi ally until King Michael I of

Romania led a successful coup against the Axis politicians and joined the Allies, with the Soviets occupying them after the war and putting a *firm socialist imprint* on the country.)

The Romanians actually had a few piston-driven, night-fighter aircraft, as noted in the story, but again, desperately out of date by now. Doves, attempting to bother hungry hawks. And about as useful.

That was why I set up the story encounters the way I did. Letting the reader look at what things would have been like in that era.

Interestingly, the MiG-15 never got a radar making it capable of operating at night. The MiG-17P (Samolet SP-7, "Fresco B") was the first, but not until much later. And the Yakovlev Yak-25 won't be introduced until 1955.

Put simply, the Soviets didn't have night-fighter capabilities at this point, and won't for a few years. That let the UN forces operate better during the Korean War, because they had all manner of aircraft that could strike in darkness and hunt.

And it will make the night skies above Yugoslavia an interesting place, because the only American jet capable of holding its own against the MiG-15 in a dogfight doesn't have radar or night-fighter equipment either.

What they have is the Red Branch.

Shade and sweet water,
blaze
West of the Mountains, WA
April 2025

PART ONE
CALIFORNIA

Dolga entered the office, noting the raw taste of cheap cigarettes in the air like a smoke cloud. It infected every surface, adding a layer of grease she suspected was entirely in her mind, but she would still wash everything when she left.

It was a dour office, occupied by a dour man who somehow managed to be half in and half out of shadow, even as he sat at his own deck, a single lamp turned sideways so artfully that the scene might have come from a movie.

Save that Comrade Morozov was not that type. He was the spider, patiently sitting at the center of a web, listening to every note and vibration as things moved around him.

In hushed tones, this Moscow building was referred to as *The Centre*. Certainly the core of the intelligence apparatus of the Soviet Union. Its nerves reached out every which way like spider silk to touch every facet of life and hear every secret whispered.

Dolga stepped in and came to rest, at attention. Neither were members of the Soviet Armed Forces, but the MGB, the *Ministry of State Security*, had taken many aspects of military life and adapted them. The Ministry of State Security had once been the NKVD, the *People's Commissariat for Internal Affairs*, until it merged uneasily with the GRU, *Military Intelligence*, though that was wisely being disassembled again today.

Comrade Morozov studied her for a long moment.

"Sit," he announced in a voice that had no more color than his pallid skin. "Close the door."

Dolga took the chair and isolated them from the rest of Centre.

They studied each other for a brief time.

"You understand the complexities of the mission, Comrade Leninova?" Morozov asked.

Dolga Leninova. *Dutiful Daughter of Lenin*. Her parents had been great supporters of the October Revolution, her sister named Oktobriana. They had never been important, but had raised two daughters through civil war, strife, purges, invasion, and peace.

"I am bait, Comrade Morozov," Dolga replied with an even nod.

Dolga knew she did not fit the propaganda image of the New Soviet Woman, being a Golden Horde descendant. Mongolian features and black hair dominated. Short and curvy. Skin more golden than western pale. Dark eyes that she had heard accused of being possessed by a black fire.

Dolga could not dispute that.

"Correct," Morozov replied. "We have not gotten all of the details, but the Red Branch somehow annihilated an entire deep-cover GRU team stationed near Los Angeles, without the assistance of the Americans. Thus far, our own spies in place have been as of yet unable to fill in the details."

Dolga nodded primly. Sat primly. Head erect. Spine straight. Hands in lap.

Quiet and harmless.

More than one fool had even fallen for such a trap.

She waited. Dolga was exceptional at waiting. Especially for answers. Especially after a decade.

"Tito has broken with Comrade Stalin," Morozov continued after a long beat and his own nod. "Much of his air force defected when he did, taking many of their aircraft with them and flying them to Hungary or Romania before returning here. Loyalty to the Party over the charismatic deviations of a fool. Yugoslavia represents a breach. A hole in that famed Iron Curtain separating East from West. What does that imply, Comrade?"

Dolga understood that she should have committed the entire mission file to memory in order to answer such a question.

And had.

"The Americans, moreso than the British or the French, will seek to exploit such a gap," she replied. "They will ply Tito with gifts and friendship, especially after failed harvests recently, hoping to peel off that land from Communism and show the world a hollow propaganda victory that they will no doubt crow about to all other nations considering splitting. Or joining the movement. Does my mission engage Tito or his partisans at any point?"

"It should not, but you must be prepared in case it does," Morozov said, possibly even smiling so fast that she missed it.

Dolga presumed that the spider across the desk from her was incapable of such emotion. Of most emotions. Of being human.

She wondered about herself, but then odd memories would bubble to the surface, bringing with them a rage that had once passed, then been rekindled.

Betrayal, then and now.

"I am prepared to contact the Red Branch, once they arrive, Comrade Morozov," Dolga replied. "There are currently five different contingency plans sketched out for completion, ranging from tactical failure to complete victory."

"Kryvenko has proven to be a far more dangerous foe than anyone understood," Morozov noted dryly. "Iron nerves. Inestimable luck. And comrades that have all been shown to be diamonds hidden in the rough. Whoever recruited that force and funded Nazarenko bottled lightning, as they say in the West. That they have done all these things in less than two years speaks to that. And others have taken notice."

"Will Tito really recruit them to defend Yugoslavia?" she asked.

"They are mercenaries, comrade," he said. "As ex-Soviet citizens, they are both welcomed there and better equipped to deal with what they find than any American might be. Plus, they are not Americans. Nor British. Exiles and enemies of the State, but it has been decreed that Moscow will use honey to woo Tito back first. We can always resort to the hammer later, if necessary. The Soviet Union will file official complaints, then ignore the Red Branch entirely. There will be some provocations, but none of the friendly neighbors have jet aircraft of any kind."

"And the new Strix they are flying is said to be at the cutting edge of such things," Dolga noted. "Is it better than the new MiG-15?"

"Without flying against it, we cannot know," Morozov shrugged. "Kryvenko and Zhidkov have both test flown the MiG, so we must presume that they will have passed along certain things to the Americans. Other departments are currently assigned to discover that information, and it does not impact on your mission."

Zhidkov. Comrade Commissar Ivan Zhidkov.

Vanya.

It had been a decade. Since before the Great Patriotic War. She had been so young. And thirty today was hardly old. Mature, perhaps.

Filled with rage and unanswered questions.

"You were chosen, Comrade Leninova, because of your connection to the Red Branch," Morozov acknowledged. "A connection that predates the war, and thus affirms that you were not tainted by the betrayals that saw those Red Branch pilots and crew exiled. Are you prepared to confront your old lover?"

"We were never lovers, Comrade," she corrected him, perhaps a trifle sharper than necessary. "He was my mentor. My teacher. The one who had begun to shape me into what I am today, before it became necessary to transfer him lateral as a Commissar for pilots and send me to the First Directorate."

Morozov watched, cold and implacable.

"And your feelings on the man today, Leninova?" he asked.

"I will return Zhidkov to Moscow," Dolga replied. "Dead or alive."

CHAPTER 2

Sasha found it hard to adjust to a new Radar Operator, but he understood the need. They had added new pilots to the Red Branch and needed to train them as much in culture as technology.

Here, though, Sasha had the advantage. Behind him sat Alfie Hirano, apparently a fourth generation native of California whose ancestors had come from Japan. Thoroughly American, for all he appeared as a small, thin, Japanese gentleman.

And smart. Possibly as intelligent as Junior Sergeant Dmitri Yefimov, distant cousin to the war hero and the team's technical genius. A high bar to clear, but Hirano had been studying for a degree in electrical engineering when Japan attacked and had taken the option to join the 442nd Regimental Combat Team. American Nisei warriors who had been one of the most decorated American units—and soldiers—in the previous war.

And, being American, he had an almost instinctive understanding of the new radar systems that Kelly had installed on the new Strix jets, the former XF-90 penetration fighter design that had proven inadequate as a high-altitude interceptor, being too heavy when designed.

Far more than merely adequate at medium levels with the new British engines. Exceptional as attack craft, where the thicker air down low usually made the work so much harder.

"Coming about," Sasha announced on the radio.

Two new pilots today as well. Both recently joined. Both recently certified. Both war veteran pilots with exceptional skills and recommendations.

Still strangers.

Sasha kicked the new Red-1 over onto the right wing, accelerating. The old XF-90 design had tried to make do with the Westinghouse J34-WE-15 jets, underpowered and unreliable. The Strix possessed Armstrong Siddeley Sapphires. Nearly double the thrust. Enough to challenge nearly any aircraft in the sky, save for perhaps a MiG-15 in the hands of a top-notch pilot.

There were not many of those around. At least not yet.

"Red-4, what is your status?" Sasha asked, still mentally summoning the fortitude to hear someone other than Pavel answer that call-sign.

"We're alright, Commander," *Beau* answered. "Having a marvelous time today."

Former RAAF Flight Sergeant Cecil Warwick. Nickname *Beau* for the Bristol Beaufighter the man had flown in the South Pacific against the Japanese.

Australian. A bit loud. A great deal boisterous. Possibly as good at low-level insertion and bombing as Lyuba. Certainly close to her in skill and a welcome addition, once Sasha had decided to expand the ranks of the Red Branch.

He would need that with the mission coming up.

They had gotten famous. For all the wrong reasons, but

there was nothing Sasha could do about that save keep driving forward.

Certainly, his ability to hunt Nazis in South America had been limited, at least for now. And the Werewolf Legion had vanished entirely for the moment.

They would return. Of that, Sasha had no doubts.

But he had somehow become a symbol of freedom. Of doing the right thing, regardless of personal costs.

Twice, they had saved America, preventing both New York City and Washington, D.C. from being bombed.

Now, quiet elements of the American government had reached out and hired the Red Branch to do something perhaps nobody else in the world was equipped to handle. Mercenaries, not beholden to any government, though an Australian and a Brit added to a team of Ukrainians and Russians would potentially be perhaps volatile.

Speaking of.

"Red-6, how are you doing?" Sasha asked as he tipped his night owl Strix over and started a slow dive.

"Jolly good, sir," Seabrook-Easton replied. "Flies so much cleaner and smoother than the Meteor or the Vampire."

UK RAF Flight Lieutenant Graham Seabrook-Easton. Had unfortunately earned the nickname *Devonshire*, the result of being the third son of the Earl Taleford, located somewhere in western England not far from Exeter. County Devon. Like *Beau*, a combat veteran of the war, with the added advantage of several years experience flying jets.

Sasha smiled. He cut the outside line to talk to Alfie Hirano, seated behind him. *Beau* had Nikon. *Devonshire* was flying with Ilya.

"Alfie, your thoughts?" he asked his new back seat assistant.

"The new experimental AN/APG-36 all-weather radar is

really exceptional, sir," Alfie replied. "Permission to chase a couple of civilian aircraft?"

"Why?" Sasha asked the man.

"The mission briefing suggests mostly propeller aircraft, if we run into someone in the sky, sir," Alfie replied with a grin. "Thus, slower than us. Less maneuverability. Less everything. We have been chasing F-86 Sabres around. And F-94s that form a portion of this aircraft design. I think we'd be well served with practice against older aircraft of a generation or two ago."

And that was why Sasha had hired the man. Smart. Insightful. Another one that might make a good team sergeant next to Ilya at some point, though neither seemed to want to pilot today.

Perhaps later.

"Excellent idea," Sasha replied, then opened up the main line. "Red-4 and Red-6, stand by to run a couple of intercept missions. All weapons are to be LOCKED DOWN. Repeat, locked down. This is merely a fly-by for training."

He got their acknowledgments and nosed around towards the south. The Los Angeles basin, just over the mountains and not that far away. Several civilian airports, to the west, the east, and the south.

And Edwards Air Force Base, the former Muroc, behind him, monitoring everything.

Nobody said anything, so he let his new team members run a little loose.

Time to better learn who they were.

CHAPTER 3

Lyuba generally managed to suppress her disdain for American sexism. To them, it was so systemic that they were generally oblivious of the words coming out of their mouths. Even Kelly, much as she loved and respected the man, was a man in a man's world, and a bit blind at times.

So she had evicted him from the room to talk to the new employee that Kelly had brought on. The Lockheed Corporation had its Skunk Works, some inside joke that she still didn't fully understand. Those teams build special aircraft for the government, as well as designing next generations of things to compete for larger military contracts.

The Red Branch had upset many plans. Worse, the new American Central Intelligence Agency had decided to get involved, with a seemingly bottomless well of money to experiment.

The new F-90B Strix was just the first example, with only a dozen built so far and half of those in long-term storage while the team readied to travel overseas. Sasha was wisely growing things slowly.

As slowly as the Americans would allow him.

At the same time, the CIA had insisted that Kelly Johnson open a second shop, even more secretive, to try really experimental designs. Things that the Red Branch could test pilot with plausible deniability later as they worked things out.

Thus, Lyuba and a much younger woman in the base wardroom, with coffee. And the local stewards had been instructed to keep everyone out while she worked. Including Kelly and Sasha.

Lyuba studied the stranger. Highly recommended. Newly graduated from Purdue University in Indiana. The School of Mechanical and Aeronautical Engineering. A unicorn, as far as all the men were concerned, because Eloise was trained as an aeronautical engineer. Like Lyuba.

"Dassau, Germany?" Eloise clarified, gesturing to the piles of documents on the table between them. "All of this paperwork?"

Lyuba nodded.

"The American Army arrested Brunolf Baade at an outsourced Junkers design office in Raguhn in April, 1945," Lyuba nodded. "They then comprehensively looted the Junkers library and took every technical document they could lay hands on, along with all the latest aircraft and engines that their soldiers could remove. Those got carted up and shipped off to New Jersey as part of some secret project I have only heard alluded to, but not been given any specific details. I do know that everything the Germans were doing at the end—every aircraft design that had gotten as far as a mockup—was captured, and at least one example shipped home."

"But this?" Eloise asked, gesturing to the stack of blueprints, rolled and unrolled at one end of the table.

"The Junkers JU-287," Lyuba replied, pulling out one tube and unrolling it. "When the Red Army was awarded control of

Dassau, they ordered all of the former Junkers employees to write down everything they could remember, then turned those men into a design bureau and attempted to replicate the 287. The EF-130 was an exact copy from leftover parts and such. The EF-140 was an updated design that they were testing in 1948, before the Soviet government shut the project down."

"Why?" Eloise asked sharply. "What went wrong?"

Lyuba shrugged.

"Possibly politics," she said. "The men who run the design bureaus are worse than hens and forever backstabbing one another over personality. I have seen some designs that would have been far better than anything anybody in the world had at the time, but the grand old men of Moscow quashed them. When Kelly mentioned that he had access to the Junkers library, I asked for someone who could take advantage of it. And they sent you."

She didn't mention that she might have yelled a bit about backwards thinking and sexist overtones, but Kelly was generally more ignorant on the topic than malevolent. He wanted the smartest people. That colleges rarely graduated women in technical fields was their fault, not his, but there were still few women. Especially since Purdue was apparently intent on evening the odds.

Eloise studied her for another moment, then unrolled the tube in her hands. Aircraft blueprints.

"Forward swept wings," Eloise mused aloud. "Rear sweep is normally necessary for breaking the sound barrier, because it delays compression. I presume that a forward sweep would do the same. Probably improves control at low speed, so landing would be easier. A few people have talked about variable geometry, wings that move through a full series of locations, allowing you to optimize for the flight envelope."

Lyuba pulled out a file folder and rifled around until she found the picture she wanted. Big twin engines hung under the wings. Bulbous nose with a lot of glazing. Tricycle under-carriage.

Smooth and clean.

Lyuba sat back and watched the woman work and think, moving back and forth across several other documents, blueprints, and pictures. Finally, Eloise looked up.

"What are we aiming for?" she asked.

Lyuba smiled at the *we*. Eloise Cutter came across as a woman used to fighting for her way. Having to be twice as good as a man to be considered anywhere close to his equal.

It was a feeling Lyuba understood well.

"New engines," Lyuba replied. "I presume that the forward sweep allows a bomb bay exactly at the center of gravity without the wing spar intruding. Some of the designs have many guns, but our own Camel only had a fixed cannon forward and a tail turret."

"Power the turret with remote controls," Eloise said firmly. "Put the gunner up front, possibly paired with the Navigator or make that a joint role. Pilot and copilot. Flight engineer, who might also be copilot. Bombardier, who might be navigator. Crew between three and five, I think. What are my limits?"

"Your expertise will analyze these designs and see what might be buildable with current technology," Lyuba replied. "There are notes on wing-warping problems the Germans ran into, but that might be as much poor quality control in the factory as a design failure. How do we offset or fix it?"

"Fuel in the wings," Eloise replied instantly. "Maybe wingtip tanks added. Engines in pods under the wings instead of inside the root like the British tend to prefer, so that they can be updated later as better become available. And pods means I can move them around as we start wind-tunnel testing."

"Kelly has a budget," Lyuba told her. "You're part of a new team he is building out, separate from the current one and working entirely under the table for the US government rather than Lockheed, I'm given to understand. Our Camel was a clean design for a medium bomber. The British are doing similar things. The Soviets are generally behind in building, because they spend more time in food fights than design meetings. How does the Red Branch get clear out to the edge of the envelope, then push that forward?"

Eloise studied her for a long moment. Lyuba waited. Finally the woman spoke.

"I'm twenty-four, Gradskaya," she began. "Isn't that young to be heading up a project like this?"

"None of the men have much more experience with jets than you do," Lyuba countered. "Except Kelly and a few. Plus, they will be forever stuck in *how we used to do it*, rather than inventing the future of aviation. I want fresh minds unafraid to ask questions."

"Like a forward-swept medium to heavy bomber?" Eloise asked. "What about the B-45 with the straight wing or the B-47 Stratojet with its sweep?"

"Conservative," Lyuba replied disdainfully. "Probably useful if you have to build hundreds of them. We need a handful at most. Really, only one that can fly high enough and fast enough to operate as an airborne command post for Yuri when his Camel is outdated. And maybe drop bombs if it comes to that. If the design works, perhaps it gets license-built elsewhere, but the Red Branch will lead the way."

Eloise shrugged.

"Making no promises, but I'll do what I can," she said.

"And the pay's far better than anything in the Midwest, for all that Chuck bitches."

Her husband. Leland, but everybody called him Chuck. Big man. Lyuba had met him once. Filled with joy and bonhomie. Those two made a good match. Lyuba needed the woman's brains and Chuck apparently made her smile.

"When we get home, I'm hoping you have something we can blackmail Kelly and the CIA into building for us."

"I'll want to fly in it," Eloise said. "Might even need to design something smaller, fighter-craft sized, to test things in the air before we go full."

"You tell me," Lyuba smiled. "We have the Strix, but it had been my experience that every year someone completely upends aviation with some new aircraft design. Only because the governments have to build them in air fleet sizes do they not all constantly stay at the bleeding edge. The Red Branch is not so limited."

"And I have access to all this?" Eloise asked, picking up a different project notebook marked Convair XA-44/XB-53 on the edge, underneath another stack labeled Boeing 449.

"All of it," Lyuba nodded. "What can we build?"

"Just watch me," Eloise grinned.

CHAPTER 4

Gennadi had settled into his role as Red Branch Command. And they had likely given up Ireland forever at this point, the Irish government quietly throwing a diplomatic hissy fit that England-based aircraft—however much a deeper investigation had suggested more Soviet agents—had attacked Irish soil intentionally.

They'd gotten angry enough during the war. Churchill's offhand suggestions that the British should have fully occupied the Irish Republic had made him no friends. As the current leader of the Opposition, he might yet return as Prime Minister, which might be an entirely different sort of catastrophe, but one Gennadi would deal with when it came.

But Ireland was done. And, Gennadi was finally willing to admit, the warm climate of Southern California had greatly lessened his aches and pains, leftovers from nearly dying at the end of the Great Patriotic War. He hardly needed the cane as anything but an affectation these days.

Apparently, Moscow cold and Dublin gloom could be cured with California sun.

At least he would remain here while Sasha took the rest on

their first political mission. Private wars between South American oligarchs didn't count.

He was out walking today, enjoying the winter sun and clear skies. Sasha kept pace beside him. Gennadi wasn't planning to walk to the far end of the runway, however many kilometers that might be, but it gave them a privacy that Gennadi couldn't take for granted in the middle of an American Air Force base.

At some point, he supposed, he needed to invest in land to build his own air facility. Probably somewhere around here, where he could be close enough to both Kelly Johnson and Edwards Air Force Base, assuming the Red Branch stayed on good terms with the US government.

"How real is the Tito/Stalin split?" Sasha was asking. "Is Yugoslavia really going to break away from the Soviet Union?"

"I have been out of the loop on political affairs for a few years, Sasha," Gennadi replied. "But Tito drove out the Germans largely on his own. Hungary and Romania were Nazi allies, so their occupation will be brutal enough to punish them, but Yugoslavia borders on Italian soil and the Adriatic, so they have more flexibility."

"And Stalin will allow such a challenge to his authority?" Sasha pressed, somewhat surprised.

Gennadi looked around before answering. Even here, in the middle of nowhere, with open flat terrain all directions. You could never be sure, and Sasha hadn't slung a machine gun on his back today.

"Stalin is old," Gennadi replied. "The maneuvering to replace him has started getting ugly. That was the exact cover story that let us create the Red Branch, one of many purges, with worse ones coming."

"Worse?"

"Nobody likes Beria," Gennadi said darkly. "There are rumors of sexual atrocities that beggar the mind. Molotov or Khrushchev are most likely to rise when Stalin goes, but nothing is guaranteed. Tito, however, has found solid theoretical grounds upon which to challenge."

"Oh?" Sasha asked.

Gennadi knew that the man was widely read and deeply educated, but had largely been intellectual about it, instead of diving deep into Marxist theory and Stalinism in detail.

"Tito advocates for a minimalist state, with power pushed down to the lowest Soviets and factory committees," Gennadi grinned. "Marx and Lenin's *Withering of the State Apparatus* that is utterly unlike anything Stalin has done in his thirty years."

"Comrade Stalin has consolidated all power in himself," Sasha noted dryly. "A new imperial dynasty, of which he was the second emperor after the Romanovs were destroyed?"

"A remarkably astute observation," Gennadi nodded. "And accurate, from a historical standpoint. Marx, no doubt, is attempting to claw his way back from hell to strangle the man."

He liked the moment of panic in Sasha's eyes before the man got the joke. If it was a joke. One could never be too sure.

"And the attempted coup?" Sasha asked.

"Summer, 1948," Gennadi nodded. "Colonel General Arso Jovanović rolled the dice and lost. Then he was killed by Yugoslav border guards while trying to escape to Romania with men like Vlado Dapčević and Branko Petričević. Tito is utterly dominant as a result, having purged his enemies as effectively as Stalin ever did."

"Gulag?" Sasha pressed.

"Islands in the Adriatic that he uses as political prisons," Gennadi said. "I doubt that you need to worry about them, as

Tito is seeking both to hire the Red Branch to act as symbolic protectors for a time, as well as to start training his people on jets."

"They will not buy the Strix, will they?" Sasha seemed surprised.

Gennadi laughed.

"No, surplus Meteors like Argentina," he said. "Or Vampires like everyone else. Your job is to buy everyone time to decide what will happen to Yugoslavia."

"We cannot stop an invasion by Red Army divisions," Sasha countered.

"And that is why you will be based initially out of the Free City of Trieste," Gennadi agreed. "That, and Yugoslav air bases continue to be attacked by Stalinesque partisans and presumably MGB or GRU operatives. Plus, Trieste Zone A is administered largely by the Americans and British, so it is somewhat safer. It is still an interesting case study in what the future might bring, save that the Soviet Union refuses to allow it to operate effectively."

"Will it return to Italy, then?" Sasha asked.

Gennadi shrugged.

"You will be surrounded on all sides by spies, double agents, fools, and charlatans, Sasha," he offered. "But that is nothing new, and you will hopefully provide the basis for a type of peacekeeping that should keep the Soviet Union from reacting badly."

"We will do what we can, Gennadi."

Gennadi nodded. It would be enough to buy time.

Or rope.

You never knew with fools.

CHAPTER 5

Vanya had acquired a new set of binoculars at the same time that Arkadi had upgraded his weapon. It was still a Winchester Model 70 design, but Arkadi had apparently had conversations with certain gunsmiths and marksmen, and his new weapon fired the .375 H&H Magnum instead. Much heavier than the 30.06 Springfield cartridge. More accurate. More deadly.

Today, they were confirming that the scope was centered exactly. According to the experts, if he was zeroed ten centimeters high at one hundred meters, it would be dead accurate at two hundred meters and hit twenty-five centimeters low at three hundred.

Far more effective than the old rifle. Far more surgical, as Arkadi had his scope configured such that five hundred meters was hittable with a bit of mathematics.

Vanya adjusted his headphones as Arkadi cycled the bolt and aimed. Bang, and another hole appeared in the center of the target at two hundred meters, today's accuracy challenge. One more shot and Arkadi was done.

Through the glass, there was only one hole in the target.

Something Vanya could cover with his thumb. At two hundred meters. It was good.

Arkadi nodded. The man rarely spoke. Sniper was as much a state of mind as anything. Sit quietly in a distant corner and wait for your prey.

"You are smiling, Vanya," Arkadi noted as he stood up and lifted Vanya to his feet.

"It takes me back," Vanya said. "To the early days of the war."

"Were you still a commissar then?"

"I was," Vanya nodded as they moved back to the bench where Arkadi had his tools.

They had the range mostly to themselves today, the guards around here generally not needing much marksmanship experience. Vanya watched Arkadi clean everything carefully before returning it to the carry bag. Precise hands.

"On the day the Germans invaded, they largely annihilated the Air Forces on the ground, bombing and strafing many units out of existence. The Air Forces had to train as many pilots as they could, rapidly, even as factories had to be picked up and shipped east of the Urals for safety. I was a commissar with land forces then and got offered a position flying. I ended up doing both, because those units would only respect someone who flew with them. Men who stayed safe at base were derided as cowards."

"And you survived the entire war," Arkadi noted with a touch of wonder.

But then, all of them had. Arkadi had been at Leningrad for a time, hunting other snipers and playing quiet games in the ruins of that great city.

"I did," Vanya noted. "But there are times I look back and wonder how things might have turned out otherwise."

"Oh?"

Arkadi paused, then slung the bag on his shoulder and nodded them into motion. Vanya followed.

"I might have remained with other portions of the government," Vanya offered. Not evasively, but leaving out certain details that might upset the others. After all, he had been with the NKVD early in his career, hunting foreign spies as ruthlessly as deviationists and backsliders.

After the war, he had not gone back, remaining with the Air Forces and occasionally test piloting things because Vanya knew his background was impeccable when it came to being trusted by higher authorities.

Occasionally, he wondered how some of his old comrades viewed him. What lurid stories they might have made up to try to understand how Comrade Commissar-Captain Ivan Zhidkov had come to be purged as a counter-revolutionary.

And they would never know the truth, likely. Not if his mission with the Red Branch was successful. It would take failure for the lies to be set correct, which made him smile.

As they emerged from the shooting zone to the parking lot, a second Jeep was parked next to theirs, with a pair of MPs waiting. The passenger even saluted, which still caused Vanya to pause, as both he and Arkadi were in the blue of the Red Branch and not the blue of the new US Air Force.

"Commander *Cernunnos* sent us, sir," the man said sharply. "There's been an update to flight orders and you are to return to headquarters immediately for a meeting."

"We will follow you back," Vanya said, noting the way the early afternoon sun was starting to stretch and turn red. Still winter, but California did not get snow at low elevations, merely turning as brutally cold as a Moscow winter at night, however dry.

Vanya drove. Arkadi watched. They offset on a wing to remain out of the dust of the jeep preceding them, covering the few kilometers back to the buildings where the Red Branch had been settled for the last six months.

Already, Vanya could see where things were nearly done being boxed up. Where trucks would carry them to a port, then a ship would haul them through the Panama Canal and the Pillars of Heracles.

The Free Port of Trieste. Vanya still was not certain if breaking down all nations into cities and hinterlands was a good idea or a poor one. He supposed that it would require a world order that could prevent men like Stalin or Tojo or Mussolini from deciding to pull it all back together into another Roman Empire. Or Soviet one. What could Europe be like if Stalin didn't feel the need to dominate a deep buffer of nations to keep the German or French from invading?

The Mongols would likely never be a serious threat again, but that was China and Russia standing on their necks to make sure. And China might fully disintegrate, in spite of everything Mao was doing to eliminate the ancient culture and create an entirely new one to replace it.

Or perhaps because of that, as Mao had all the hallmarks of another Stalin. Another Communist Emperor at the head of a new imperial dynasty.

Old Vanya would have happily crushed Tito's deviationist tendencies. Today, he was going to help protect an experiment in what Marx had originally been preaching. Even Lenin had expected the opposite of what had happened under Stalin.

Thus, Trieste and Yugoslavia represented a possible new future that might make the world truly a better place.

If he could protect it from emperors.

CHAPTER 6

Sasha looked over his newly expanded team. Ukrainian. Russian. Australian. English. American.

The United Nations, united in this room, trying to make the world a better place.

Gennadi had taken a seat off to one side of the second row, making sure Sasha was central. Nobody in the room that was not one of them. Wearing the Stag's Head logo.

Even the ground crews that the Air Force and Lockheed had quietly hired were not in this room for this meeting. Only the Red Branch.

Sasha watched expectant faces for a long moment before speaking, understanding that a new future had arrived. One he was certain Gennadi and his bosses had never imagined.

One Sasha was tasked with implementing.

"A contract has been signed," he began simply, momentous in spite of himself, because his signature committed them.

Thrust the Red Branch into the center of things, attempting to hold a vaguely understood no-man's-land while titans paused and glowered at each other from the corners.

Something other than war, which he had already risked his life too many times already to prevent.

"Tomorrow, at first light, we will launch in sequence, headed east," Sasha continued. "The Camel has been refitted to handle aerial refueling from pods on the wings and internal tanks, but the Strix should be able to make each hop successfully. From here to a base near Detroit. Then on to St. John, Newfoundland, where we will spend the night. From there, over the Atlantic to Cork in Ireland, before finally flying over the Bay of Biscay, southern France, the Mediterranean Sea, and the Italian peninsula to land directly at Trieste, where air facilities are being provided by our American hosts. We will fly patrols and training missions over Yugoslavia but will remain based in the Free City for now."

"Are we likely to travel to Belgrade or Sarajevo?" *Beau* asked, eyes aglitter with possibilities.

"If we do, it will be under controlled circumstances," Sasha replied, smiling grimly. "Yugoslavia is rather famous for the quality of their partisans, and not all of them support Tito's current government. In fact, the reason for basing out of Trieste is that Tito's air bases keep getting hit by those same partisans. As some of you can testify, if you lose base security, all sorts of mischief can occur."

That got a laugh. Most of them had helped him break into the Werewolf Legion base and steal the Silver Eagle. He shuddered at trying to hold a base with what those Paraguayan troops had considered security.

At least the Americans were very serious about holding the line. Their reasons might be questionable, but not the seriousness of their intent. Not today.

"You have read the briefings," he continued. "As in South America, do not assume that anyone you meet is what they appear to be. If you have questions, contact your pilot or bring it directly to me. We have enemies and will be far closer to them tomorrow than I had originally intended. At the same time, notice has quietly been given that everyone else is trying to find a way to handle the situation without overt violence."

"Provocations, either in the sky or on the ground?" Lyuba asked.

"Without doubt," Sasha nodded. "We will fly in pairs or triads or even the full team. The Strix can take anything else in the sky, at least in your hands. MiG-15s might be a challenge, but they are not on this frontier, as far as I am aware, so unless the Soviet Union steps up those provocations, we should be facing military ordnance leftover from the war. All propeller driven and not even that fast or that dangerous, save in numbers."

"Do we use force?" *Devonshire* asked crisply.

"We will be patrolling the skies of Yugoslavia as their defenders," Sasha stated. "If someone comes across a border, we will intercept and investigate. And yes, we will be armed and prepared to down them."

"Not just chase them off, sir?" *Beau* pressed.

"They will have come looking for a fight, *Beau*," Sasha said. "We will give it to them if they demand it."

Sasha made a point of pulling his shoulders back down and relaxing them. Still, he looked around at everyone and got sober nods. Serious business.

"In that case, let us review our flight plans, then we will head to an early dinner..."

PART TWO
THE FREE CITY

Yuri could only keep up with the owls when they were flying slow and he was pushing. Still, they had hung back some, coming across the Adriatic. Six aircraft, with him at the tip of an arrowhead like geese flying northeast.

"Yuri, I'm picking up signals from our right," Dmitri called from forward, where the bombardier's station had several radar additions, intended to make the Camel an airborne command post. "You owe me."

Yuri nodded and shrugged. He had indeed bet the man that nobody would attack them over the neutral airspace of the Adriatic.

And yes, probably been wrong.

"What do you have?" Yuri asked.

"Twelve signals, grouped in three flights of four," Dmitri replied. "Closing at about six hundred kph. Above us somewhat, probably preparing to swoop. Do these fools not understand that we have radar?"

"Day fighters?" Yuri asked. "Remember, only nightfighters like the Strix usually have radar, to say nothing of converted bombers like ours. They might be expecting less capable aircraft."

He ignored Dmitri's professional grumbles and opened the team radio frequency.

"All Red Branch aircraft, this is Red-5," he announced. "Radar has detected inbound aircraft at zero-nine-zero with a hostile flight profile. Stand by to engage. Red-1, you have command."

CHAPTER 8

Somehow, Sasha had known.

Deep in his bones, where instinct had kept him alive more times than he admitted, a voice had whispered that someone would attempt something here, at the very end. The Strix were not out of fuel, but a sudden dogfight would probably come close to emptying tanks if he let it go on for long.

And here, with blue water below and Italy to his left hemisphere and Yugoslavia in the near distance ahead and to starboard, Yuri and Dmitri had apparently spotted trouble.

Neutral waters. Neutral air. Who would attack them?

Albania came immediately to mind, but he also knew that Tito and Hoxha were polite, if mortal, enemies, the one breaking from Stalinism and the latter demanding that Yugoslavia toe the line.

He could see an Albanian squadron attempting...something. Twelve on five did not look like fair odds. Six with the Camel.

But the Red Branch flew state of the art combat jets. Had Stalin slipped a force of MiGs in anyway?

"Red Branch, this is *Cernunnos*," he called. "Stand by to

come about onto heading one-three-five. Radar operators, begin tracking. All pilots, unlock your weapons."

Early in the war, the 12.7mm machine gun—the famous American Fifty—had been sufficient, though armor and better designs later had made them underpowered. Twenty millimeter cannon had replaced them in western aircraft, and the twenty-three millimeter NR-23 in recent Soviet designs. And the Nightvipers.

Because Kelly had built and customized new aircraft for the Red Branch, Gennadi had used his confused British contacts to acquire sets of 30 mm ADEN revolver cannons when he got engines. Perhaps excessive, but until someone actually built a missile capable of successfully homing in on an enemy aircraft in a dogfight, it would come down to better pilots and better aircraft.

The Strix was, as far as Sasha knew, the best in the air right now.

"Coming around now," Sasha announced. "Red-5, stand by to move to castle position."

Yuri flew a maneuverable medium bomber, but he had no business in a dogfight, regardless of his opinions on the topic. Though the Camel could bite if anyone did bother him.

The sun had been behind him somewhat. Now it was more in his face. No doubt those enemy aircraft had been expecting to catch him unaware, not knowing how good his radar systems were.

Or their operators.

"Enemy aircraft flying at roughly three hundred and seventy knots," Alfie announced. "One thousand feet above us. Uhm. Hang on. Six hundred twenty-five kph. Three hundred meters above."

Sasha grinned but didn't say anything. The Americans used

British measurements, generally. Feet and miles. But this was a European unit, so everything was metric. And Alfie would learn. Was learning. Was actually brilliant, but hadn't flown combat before today, having only been shot at in an Italian foxhole, somewhere south of where the Red Branch had recently overflown.

"*Cernunnos*, Albania flies Yak-9 aircraft," Lyuba—*Banshee*—called over the line. "Usually armed with one ShVAK in twenty millimeter and a pair of 12.7mm UBS machine guns on the wings. Flight characteristics suggest they are configured for long-range escort duties instead of bombing."

And while Alfie might be good, *Banshee* knew aircraft. All aircraft. Anywhere. Whoever.

It was nice, having a walking encyclopedia flying with them. Several of them.

"Are they seriously challenging us, mate?" *Beau* asked, confused.

"Someone might be attempting to make a statement, *Beau*," Vanya commented.

"Hope he brought a parachute," the Aussie grumbled. "Standing by to kick some arse."

Sasha grinned. That attitude was exactly why Gennadi had interviewed the man, located via common friends in Britain. *Devonshire* might have better jet skills, but *Beau* had flown at the Battle of the Bismark Sea in 1943, a brutal affair where a Japanese invasion force in convoy got slaughtered by Allied pilots using newly-invented skip-bombing techniques. Flying under one hundred meters at over three hundred kph, and literally bouncing bombs across the surface of the water to slam into the side of a transport after the fuse delay ended.

The Japanese had lost more transports and destroyers than the Allies lost aircraft in that battle. And possibly lost the war in the South Pacific there, just as Midway had crushed their aircraft carrier force and cost them the North and Central Pacific.

"Confirming Red-5's read of three quads inbound, Commander," Alfie called from the back seat of Red-1, eyes no doubt glued to screens. "No other aircraft located. Red-5, confirm your overwatch."

"Roger that, Red-1," Dmitri replied. "We have clear skies to a range of one hundred kilometers."

"Red-4, stay with me," Sasha called. "Red-6, stay on Red-2's wing. *Banshee*, you're on your own."

Lyuba's laughter probably chilled souls, if those Albanian fools were on the correct frequency to listen. But he had no doubts that Lyuba could take care of herself.

Still, Sasha could see adding Red-7 at some point, so they had three teams. And maybe another transport of some sort for Yuri. Maybe an armed fortress like the B-17 and B-29 the Americans had flown during the war. Castles in the air, as a statement, with knights on horseback sallying.

First, he had business to attend to.

CHAPTER 9

Lyuba smiled, saddened that Yanina wasn't seated immediately beside her to share the joke and perhaps roll her eyes at what *Banshee* was about to do.

"Is your harness tightened?" Yanina asked tartly from the back seat.

Lyuba laughed, then checked anyway, just in case. They had been in the air for several hours, and Kelly simply did **not** understand how to build a system that took breasts into account.

Banshee tightened everyone that last notch, then pulled back the throttle.

"Red-3, engaging," she announced, aiming her nose directly at the closing squadron of pissy chipmunks come to bother her.

Slight incline. Excessive power in the engines behind her. DURABLE aircraft because the design had predated true understanding of transsonic speeds. Everyone had thought that the stresses would be greater, so the original prototype could take twelve Gs. These models could shrug off at least six.

And had better armaments.

"Everyone stand by for me to scatter them," *Banshee* called, locating the central aircraft and aiming directly at it, then drifting her nose a little high and firing a quick burst.

Ranging fire, because they had been unable to engage aerial targets in a true dogfight. Mocks against arrogant men in Sabres, certainly, but not live cannon fire.

Nor with old Yaks.

Lyuba got lucky. The range, the wind, the enemy squadron, and even the weather conspired to fly that leader right into her burst. She watched his propeller flash several times, then disintegrate as 30mm rounds shattered the blades and the engine.

Rather than stay put as the others decided to fire back, she dove. Throttle open. Mach was accessible in this aircraft, but she had to be careful in her fuel use, so she let gravity assist instead of pushing.

And maybe, just because, flashed her tail at those silly pilots like a doe spooking and racing into the nearby woods.

How many foolish hounds would chase her?

CHAPTER 10

Vanya had *Devonshire* on his wing. Exceptional pilot with more years in jets than anybody else in the Red Branch, the British having fielded Meteors early and led most Allied technological development for a time.

When they could still afford it.

Before the bills came due and Great Britain woke up broke and hungover.

They still designed lovely aircraft, but simply couldn't afford to build them, which was a pity. The Nightviper had been fantastic to fly. Maneuverable. Intuitive. Smooth.

The Strix was growing on him, but Kelly had designed a Penetration Fighter, intended to travel deep into Soviet territory, accompanying the bombers and protecting them. Rugged. Fast because British engines powered it. And British guns.

Deadly.

Vanya watched *Banshee* flush the enemy squadron and even score a probable kill on the lead fighter. The Yaks broke like a vase dropped on the floor, with several rolling and diving to go after her. And not in pretty teams.

"Red-6, we're going high right and then rolling back and in," Vanya called.

"Got your wing, Red-2," *Devonshire* replied.

Vanya nodded and pulled back on his stick and rolled it over. Elevation. Altitude. Speed. Three of the Yaks turned to stay with him, but again, mismatched pairs because the Red Branch was opening like a flower and the Yak pilots had just lost their squadron commander, flames visible now as he tilted over.

Probably nobody issuing orders for a moment.

Vanya went hard for a corner, understanding that the old Yaks had the maneuverability, but not the speed. They turned to shoot at him, committed to the wrong vector when he and Red-6 blasted by them at high speed.

"*Ecne*, this is *Cernunnos*," Sasha called. "Take the group chasing *Banshee*. I have the ones trying to get to you."

"Roger that," Vanya replied.

One quick glance to make sure where the other groups were, then he stood on a wing, reversed hard, and dove.

Five of the Yaks had ended up going after *Banshee*. Foolish move on their part, because they lacked the speed and she was already well past them and going away.

Still, it put them in a pretty arrowhead, like geese when a giant hawk was about to pounce on them.

Vanya drifted to his right, sideslipping while keeping his nose on the three lined up on the right side.

They flew like young Soviet pilots. Following their leader's orders without any question, because that was the system Stalin had built.

Never question your superior.

It took experience to become a leader. To become someone

that others looked to for inspiration and orders. He had done it before the war. And during.

And now, as Sasha expanded their squadron, he was continuing, with *Devonshire*, the young British nobleman Graham Seabrook-Easton being all of twenty-five years old. At thirty-five, he made Vanya feel ancient.

Still, the man flew with a natural touch, exactly in position when Vanya glanced over.

"Firing," Vanya announced, walking a long burst up the line of three aircraft as he pulled delicately back on his stick and walked his aiming point.

Beside him, a string of lights as *Devonshire* did the same, occasional tracers visible even in the daylight.

The closest Yak caught a double burst and crumpled like a can run over by a lorry. One moment fine, the next shedding parts and flames.

Then Vanya was by the three and pulling back and up, rolling away to their rear where he might reverse again and catch them confused.

Upside down and looking back, they had split again, two coming after him and two more still chasing *Banshee*. No, one after *Banshee*. The second target Vanya had strafed seemed to be having troubles.

Old aircraft did not have the armor to resist 30mm fire. Thus, new generations of aircraft were necessary.

And the Yaks could not keep up.

"*Ecne*, trouble ahead," Arkadi called from the back seat.

Vanya leveled and noticed a group going after Yuri's Camel. They were losing ground as Yuri used his jets to gain altitude faster than they could, but it reminded Vanya of a carrot dangled in front of a mule.

Or a rabbit taunting the hounds.

Still, three more strung out.

"*Devonshire*, you take the straggler," Vanya ordered. "I have the leader. We'll react to the fool in the middle when he realizes we're here."

"Tally ho!"

Vanya laughed. The old British pilots hunting cry that meant something like, "Target in sight, engaging!"

And they did.

A rabbit, taunting the hounds, and distracting them from a pack of wolves emerging from the brush.

Vanya throttled back until he felt like he was walking, but that merely let him pace the Yaks chasing Yuri. And he could see where Oleg Markov, in the rear turret, was taking long-range shots. Likely intended to keep their eyes forward, because Yuri suddenly flew a line steady and true.

"NOW!" Vanya called, thumbing the firing switch on his stick.

More fire lashed out. The Yak's tail shattered, then tore off.

Devonshire had done something similar, but farther forward, because that Yak broke into two.

Someone had not done much maintenance to keep these aircraft flight-worthy? Or, as *Banshee* had noted, they had been reconfigured for long-range patrol. Had someone taken out those heavy armor plates to gain range?

Foolish.

And terminal.

The third one rolled and dove in an expert move that made him impossible to track, so Vanya let him go, pulling left to get clear of Yuri's flight path.

Oleg, it seemed, had been waiting for his moment, because Vanya caught a tail of flame emerge.

"Arkadi, how's that last one?" Vanya asked, focused on the remaining enemy fliers.

"On fire and going down," Arkadi said on the intercom. "He was looking at you and *Devonshire* was able to semi-stall on his tail. Red-6 and Red-5 crossfired him. I already have a parachute in the air."

Vanya nodded and ignored him. Yuri was in the clear and the odds had now been greatly evened out.

Time to finish the job.

CHAPTER 11

Sasha had discovered early on that he could visualize an entire aerial battle in his head and hold a dozen aircraft as they moved around. Useful, when he had begun training young pilots and needed to make sure they didn't run into one another. Or him.

Here, he was tracking groups well enough. *Banshee* had rear-footed the Albanians to open the match and was busy causing even more mayhem as their leader lost command. And his aircraft.

Possibly his life, because Sasha wasn't seeing a parachute emerge.

They had started it.

"*Beau*, stand by," he called. "Up and left, then hooking in as they react. Ignore the ones going after *Banshee* because she can outrun them."

"Japanese convoy, *Cernunnos*," *Beau* replied with a rumbling laugh.

Sasha grinned. He'd gotten *Beau* a little drunk one night and asked about that running battle.

In vino, veritas. In wine, you will hear the truth.

Beau was a better pilot than he let on. Far better. Skip-bombing Japanese destroyers firing everything they had in the few moments when they had an opportunity.

Before deadly bombs slammed into the sides of their ships.

Idly, Sasha wondered if they could acquire some torpedoes at some point, though he had no naval enemies to use them on. Yet.

Beau Warwick was still an artist. His medium was explosive destruction at low altitude.

Sasha flared wide to his left with Red-4 keeping pace. The Yaks tried to turn with him, but their formation wasn't coherent, and then he was past them, turning hard inward at stresses older aircraft like that would disintegrate under.

Four had gone after *Ecne* in their excitement, except one pair from the left group and two randoms from the other quads.

The mark of young pilots with have hardly any combat piloting experience.

Doves, sent aloft against hawks.

Gennadi, talking about the early days of the war, when experienced Luftwaffe killers took on Russian boys with a few hours of piloting under their belts.

Most had never returned to base.

Today, Sasha was the hawk.

He lined up on the rearmost of the ones failing to pace Vanya. A burst and the right hand wing was trailing flames and smoke, so Sasha slid on to the one ahead of him and watched that one pull up sharply, like he might cause the faster jet to blast by before Sasha could react.

Beau had as much combat experience as anybody in the Red Branch and crucified that Yak as though a man hung on a cross.

It came apart under the impact. The other two split right

and left. Excellent flying, but Sasha suspected that it was panic on their part and not the perfect maneuver to avoid a pair of hungry owls coming up behind them.

Then he was past them. One of the pair of Albanians was turning to chase Vanya, at half his speed, while the other was climbing.

Again, good instincts. Wrong aircraft, because the Strix had a higher ceiling. And higher speed. And better maneuverability. And bigger guns.

Sasha throttled back and rode with the man for a moment, waiting his chance.

There.

A slight drift to the left and a burst that exploded a wing instead of killing the pilot. Maybe he would survive. And learn. And become a better pilot next time.

Sasha did not wish to become a butcher. Even today.

The Yak entered a flat spin, remaining wingtip up like a car sliding somewhat sideways on ice. Sasha circled and nodded when the canopy opened and a man jumped clear.

Open sea below him, but they were close to Yugoslavia. And Italy. And an American base. Hopefully, someone had a ship or flying boat handy.

If nothing else, these men deserved a chance to make it home safe, regardless of what their commanders had ordered them to attempt.

"Alfie, where are the rest?"

CHAPTER 12

Banshee laughed and went for sky. The Strix could not go straight up but had a climb rate that put these poor Yaks to shame. Looking around as she spun, already the Yaks were in trouble and possibly doomed, the sky filled with planes on fire or in pieces as the Red Branch went to work.

For a moment, she considered being utterly cross that they had been so badly underestimated by whoever did this but that just meant that she and the others were forewarned of trouble coming next time, when their enemies had to significantly increase their attacking force.

"*Cernunnos*, this is *Banshee*," she said on the radio, even as she picked out one pilot who had realized how badly outclassed he was.

"Go ahead," Sasha replied quickly, gunfire in the background as he continued to engage the few fools left.

"Do we let the others go?" she asked, ignoring the squawk of surprise from the back seat. And the snickers that quickly followed.

Yanina understood how much terror and panic a handful

of survivors would bring back to base with them. Might infect the entire Albanian Air Force with it.

That would certainly make her job up north easier.

Banshee idled back more and more as the Yak in front of her tried to slow enough to force a stall. She had about two seconds to either engage or race away before he could get his guns around to shoot at her, though she wasn't sure what 12.7mm bullets might to do her Strix.

Kelly had designed and built them tough. And even the production models, lighter and not quite as much tanks as the prototype, were durable.

Still, best not to test that today.

"Agreed," Sasha said. "Red Branch, break off from enemy aircraft and get to altitude quickly. Let them go if they wish. We can always run them down if they stay."

Banshee nodded and pulled back, adding a quick reverse as she pointed her nose at the sky and increased throttle.

"How are we for fuel?" she asked her back seat, not wanting to look down at her console as she tracked that Yak.

Fool actually thought about coming after her for a moment, before nosing himself over and probably offering thanks to Marx and whoever else that she wasn't finishing him.

"It will be tight, but Yuri has the pods mostly full," Yanina replied. "Recommend he top us off when we have a moment."

"Understood," Lyuba said, then switched channels. "Red-5, this is Red-3, I am running low on fuel, when you have a moment."

"Roger that, *Banshee*, Yuri replied quickly. "We appear to have clearing skies. I will bring things level and slow down. You match me for speed and I will deploy the drogue for refueling."

Lyuba went ahead and deployed her probe as she located the Camel above and ahead of her.

"All Red Branch elements, this is Red-5," Dmitri announced. "Enemy squadron has broken contact. Repeat, broken contact and is currently headed away to East-South-East."

"Let them go," Sasha followed up. "Dmitri, contact coastal authorities. Italian, American, and Yugoslav on their various channels. Give them these coordinates and ask for rescue operations to deploy. There are several parachutes in the air, but we are well away from dry land."

Lyuba nodded to herself. Like spearing fish in a barrel, but only three of the original twelve were racing madly away from them. Probably asking why they had been offered up as a sacrifice, because someone had not done their homework before ordering this attack.

What would they try next?

CHAPTER 13

Dolga had selected a place to stay in Trieste with a nice view of the new air base that had been cleared and built on the remains of a German Wehrmacht armed forces base that the New Zealanders had occupied after the Nazi surrender. The Germans had held out long enough to not be taken by Tito's forces, which had probably been wise on their part.

The area around here was only slowly being rebuilt, nobody certain what would happen next. Or when. Trieste had only been Italian for a generation, and before that Austro-Hungarian. The local Slovene population had no love for either but weren't in a position to argue with the winners of the war, and Stalin had not allowed any progress to be made with permanently turning the area into a free city.

Tito, she knew, wanted to add it to Yugoslavia, but he was also maneuvering to carve off chunks of Austria while borders might yet be fluid, an ego perhaps as big as Stalin's, though she kept her opinions on the topic to herself.

Moscow was fermenting. Dolga found herself relaxed to be well away from those struggles, mostly because Centre was going to be just that. Central. The bullseye in the struggles that followed Stalin's inevitable death, thought she wasn't sure who would be holding the wooden stake when it finally happened.

Still, Western Trieste. The Free Territory. Possibly a new Freeport or tiny nation about to be born, like Monaco or Luxembourg.

The Italians had acted like shits to the Slovenes, and were not welcome here. Dolga looked Slavic enough not to be mistaken for one of Mussolini's fools, but the Americans around here were largely ignorant of such distinctions and the British tended to be even more racist than the Italians.

But everyone in Trieste simply was trying to survive. To hustle in the ruins. No different here than Berlin, last time she had been there pursuing an operation in the French sector.

She pulled her pack and lit a cigarette as her man Rade approached her, glasses of local beer in each hand. Dolga was dressed as a civilian. Perhaps a secretary meeting a man midday in some tawdry affair away from prying eyes, since he didn't look Western.

She drew a lungful of smoke as he settled.

"Any updates?" she asked quietly, surrounded and hidden by the noise of others talking.

Yesterday, the afternoon had been shattered by a half-dozen aircraft landing. Strange ones. Powerful jets.

Then the news had come out of Tirana via coded radio message.

"Three aircraft made it back to base, though one crashed when his gear failed to deploy," Rade murmured. "Rumors suggest that the Red Branch let them get away, when they could have slaughtered them."

Dolga paused to absorb that. Was it mercy on their part? Five jets and a bomber, utterly devastating a dozen old Yakolev-9 fighters.

How ruthless was her foe?

Then she smiled.

"Mistress?" Rade asked, a bit nervous, which she found even more intriguing.

He was older than her by at least a decade. Heavyset, with scarred ears from boxing and scarred hands from the war. Dark eyes that turned steel gray in the right light.

And frightened of her. Or at least First Directorate in Moscow. Wisely so.

"I wondered if they were being merciful," she said, taking a sip of the dark, bitter beer. "But then I remembered what happened in California."

"Oh?" He leaned in like whispering delights in her ear, but she knew he would recoil in terror if she joined him in a kiss.

"They slaughtered a GRU deep-cover team that tried to ambush them," Dolga nodded. "Ran over several with lorries on the highway, from the reports I have seen."

Rade blinked. Swallowed.

The Partisans had been hard men and women, but many had forgotten how to be truly ruthless. That was why she was here.

To remind them.

"They let those pilots escape, to warn the Albanian Air Force to mind their manners," she decided aloud. "I will expect that future forays against the Red Branch will be tentative, at best, as a result. And when the news gets out, pilots from the other neighbors will be equally cautious. Equally squeamish."

"Does this impact our mission?" he asked.

At the end of the day, Rade Davidović worked for her, a proud Stalinist who kept the original faith in the face of deviationism, however quietly he did in an era where Tito was rounding people up and executing the ones who challenged him.

"Only in the timing," she assured her minion. "How is Dr. Perko?"

"Still in Zagreb," Rade nodded. "Working in his lab, puttering on various projects for the moment, with everything either memorized or hidden in such a way that he could quickly flee, once he makes contact with agents here in Trieste."

Dolga smiled. Considered her timing.

"You travel directly to him," she ordered. "Meet him in person, privately, using good tradecraft to elude any watchers, **whoever** they might report to. Prepare him to remain in place for a time as the situation develops. I must transmit several messages and get replies, then begin moving pieces around. The delay will be no less than two weeks, but it is unavoidable."

"And the Red Branch will truly assist him to defect?"

Rade seemed shocked, but that was provincial ignorance. Dolga suspected that he had never traveled any further from his birth village than Trieste or Belgrade.

"They will," she assured him. "And then, I will destroy them all."

CHAPTER 14

Vanya was reminded of Moscow some, in the ways that so many armed soldiers patrolled regularly. So many checkpoints. He had never been to Berlin, but stories suggested a similarity to the Western Zones of that city as well, with Yugoslavia itself lurking just over the second range of hills from the water.

Lurking, indeed, as nobody knew what would become of Trieste. Or when.

It was a cold day. Winter still hung on, unable to decide if it would remain or blow on to Siberia. Clouds, but high up and not threatening rain. Merely chill.

Vanya wore the medium blue uniform of the Red Branch, which stood out brightly against the darker greens of the Americans or the browns and grays of civilians, hustling about with their heads down and shoulders generally hunched forward.

And against more than the cold.

He could separate the crowds around him into the proud Italians who had owned this city for a generation, and the Slovenes who had been so badly treated by Mussolini's regime.

Vanya wondered if the Americans were mostly here to keep the Italians from being slaughtered.

After all, the Wehrmacht had fought tenaciously against Tito's Partisans until the end, fearing that they would be rounded up and possibly executed for how the rest of the war had gone. It had taken the arrival of the Kiwis before the Germans surrendered.

How would the Italians hold up?

He had paused, looking across part of the city from a bit of elevation where he could see the port below. And the ships, destroyers and freighters, that kept this enclave alive. Beside him, Graham—*Devonshire*—waited politely, still getting used to the greatcoats that were necessary today. Heavy and wool, done in a manner similar to what would flood the streets of Moscow today, save that no Soviet would be so bright.

Except, perhaps, a general officer pretending to be a peacock. If they were pretending.

Vanya shrugged and grinned to himself, turning back to note Graham's hints of nervousness.

"We're safe, out and about by ourselves?" Graham asked.

Vanya nodded and began to walk, drawing the man with him. They were both armed with their Shanxi Type 17 pistols. The Mauser style pistol rebuilt entirely from scratch by a Chinese warlord in .45 caliber.

Apparently, Gennadi had located and acquired several hundred such weapons, captured by Mao's armies and willingly swapped for Soviet gear. Like the stag's head, another mark of the Red Branch.

"I doubt that we will have troubles," Vanya replied, brushing lightly past people like a salmon headed upstream. "And the Americans will know who we are soon enough. I wanted a chance to see Trieste before the locals knew us. To get a better understanding on where they want to go."

"Part of your training as a…?"

He wisely caught himself short there. Commissar was absolutely not a word to speak aloud. Not here. Not today. Trieste lived in fear that Tito would come for them. Italian Trieste, anyway. The Slovenes probably prayed for such salvation, but again, Tito had broken publicly with Stalin and that situation had gotten ugly. And could get worse if people chose that route.

Thus, Tito's willingness to hire the Red Branch as a sort of aerial peace keeping force, beholden to nobody and comfortable with all of the cultures involved.

"Yes," Vanya agreed. "Part of what I did before the war. A significant part of that job involved walking in crowds like this, studying people and making educated guesses about which ones to watch closer."

He had only been a flight commissar later. After Barbarossa had destroyed the Soviet Air Forces so abruptly. Prior to that, he had worked in other tasks. Internal and external security.

Vanya did not speak or read as many languages as Sasha, but that gap wasn't as wide as many probably presumed. Vanya simply didn't mention it often.

"What does Trieste tell you?" Graham asked in a neutral, curious voice.

Vanya started to wave him off, then reconsidered. Sasha was probably making the man over into his wingman for now, just as Sasha would keep *Beau* closer. And eventually, they would locate a pilot who could take orders from Lyuba without question or complaint, though that might require a bit more effort. Or blackmail on the part of American General Lockwood Carlyle, who had several USAF pilots he wanted to introduce.

But Graham had asked a question. A cogent one, especially from the mouth of a petty nobleman of British descent. An answer was justified, but perhaps not on the streets.

"Come, let us get some coffee," Vanya said, gesturing to a nearby cafe.

They entered and found a table in a corner, the center of attention, but Vanya glowered sufficiently that the comments were kept quiet.

Folks had probably heard that mercenaries were coming. And everyone had seen them land the other day. Today, he was, perhaps, making a statement to the city that the Red Branch had arrived, even as Sasha would be meeting with some of Tito's people about their first patrol.

A waitress approached with menus and a glass sphere of coffee, filling mugs then retreating while Vanya considered food as well. They had dollars, which would be greatly desired by the locals. Sasha saw part of their task in Trieste to inject money for recovery to the city. Rent, fuel, materials, even as they spent time aloft over nearby Yugoslavia to show the flag.

Or however it might be interpreted.

Looking around, he wondered how many languages might be spoken in just this room. It had that sort of feel. Italian, Slovenian, Serbo-Croatian, English. Who else? Probably French, given proximity. Doubtful any Arabic or Ottoman dialects but there might be a few who spoke it at home.

Still, he would stick to English, mostly because Vanya didn't speak Ancient Greek or Latin worth a damn, though Graham knew both.

And he studied his comrade closer as they sat and sipped coffee. Brown hair. Bristly mustache. Lantern jaw like a cinema hero, though built more lean than either he or Sasha. Highly intelligent. Highly recommended. A good wingman.

"The city speaks to me of two masters," Vanya began, picking up the previous conversation. "One that replaced the other after the previous war. And uncertainty about who will hold power after this one."

"Is another Monaco possible?" Graham asked.

Vanya shrugged. Considered his recent history. And the world's.

"Without the break after the war, I think it might have been welcomed in certain palaces," he replied vaguely, but watched a knowing light appear in Graham's eyes. "Certainly, the ideals of breaking down nation states and letting locals govern themselves is a noble one, but one of the neighbors has a blind spot along those lines, according to the materials we were provided before we left. If he supported it, it might happen. Since he looks to push eventually, it will probably fail."

"Revert with all those problems returning?" Graham asked.

Vanya had had his concerns about adding an English nobleman to the team. Even the third son of a minor one such as Earl Taleford. But Sasha had read the man correctly. Smart. And open-minded. And perhaps a great deal more pink than most of his peers, however quiet he might be about it.

"They did not do themselves any justice prior to the war," Vanya nodded. "Today, Zone A looks one way and Zone B the other. Those might be the final boundaries when everything is settled, one way or the other."

"Hopefully, we can prevent a war," Graham replied.

Vanya nodded. That was part of the reason the Red Branch had been sought out. Neutrality in a situation with explosive potential. The Berlin Airlift had not escalated, but Vanya would have lost any bet on that outcome.

Both sides seemed to understand that there were lines that

should be honored, though both were utterly convinced of the rightness of their own cause. If they would only set back and let that rightness convince others, instead of reaching out a greedy, grasping hand.

Vanya started to say something when a ghost walked in the door, moved to a table facing this way from less than five meters away, and smiled at him.

CHAPTER 15

Sasha studied the man he was meeting in person for the first time, all previous contacts having been via telegram and post.

Neven Ćosić. Serbian. A personal representative for Tito in Trieste, specifically something like an ambassador to the Red Branch, and a deputy to the man Tito had working with the Free City's embryonic government and the Americans.

The stranger was rail thin, with a shock of white hair and clean shaven. Average height, but an enormous personality that made him seem much taller. Almost Sasha's height.

They had shaken hands and sat, but Sasha was reminded of two boxers sent to their corners to await the opening bell.

"We have filed a formal complaint with Albania," Ćosić began. "However, as the contract for services technically came into effect at the moment your team deployed to Trieste by landing, there is little that can be done."

"Another unfortunate case of air piracy?" Sasha asked dryly.

They were speaking Russian today, though Ćosić spoke excellent English. Mostly, he wanted privacy from the Americans who surrounded him.

Or at least to make them really work at it.

Ćosić jolted.

"Yes, that would be a lovely term to describe what those sheep farmers have done," the man sneered. "Continue to do. This is not the first time there have been aerial misunderstandings. Until we can rebuild our air forces, we are at risk."

"Your commander facing war on all of his Communist frontiers?" Sasha pressed.

Hungary. Romania. Bulgaria. Albania. A Greek civil war in the south distracting them. Austria to the north preferring to be as neutral as everyone would allow. And a much-chastened Italy just over the northern frontier.

Plus a lot of American firepower within close range if things got out of hand, but someone would have to cross into Trieste proper for it to deploy, Sasha suspected.

His job was to keep all of that under control. However he had to.

"I think they would like to," Ćosić replied. "But that would be a tacit admission on their parts that Tito was right. That he had the people of Yugoslavia entirely on his side and that the only way to return my nation to the fold would be to conquer it, something they did not do during the war because we drove the Germans out ourselves."

Sasha let him have that moment. The reality, like always, had been far more complicated. But Tito's forces had tied down an impossible number of German divisions that might have made a bigger difference in the east or west as the pincers had closed inexorably in.

"What other air piracy have you faced?" Sasha asked.

Then he sat back and watched the man talk. Rant. Explain. Digress. Vent.

If it was a performance, it was an entertaining one. If it was the truth, Tito had selected someone with the fire of a true believer to convey his needs to the Red Branch. And the West.

A man like Sasha had been, once upon a yesterday. Or rather, he still was, but had gone far beyond Marx and Stalin, confronted by the modern limitations both encountered.

Night-time raids on bases, both in the air and on the ground, mostly aimed at aircraft parked and waiting. Strikes on individuals and convoys that sounded remarkably similar to what Sasha had done in South America when he first arrived, an assassination via P-47 Thunderbolt because nobody else had been in a position to stop him.

Slip across a border quickly, drop bombs on trucks or bridges, and slip back before anyone could chase them down.

"And you lack the sorts of radar systems to warn you?" Sasha asked when Ćosić took a breath.

"They would likely only become the next set of targets," the man sighed. "Destroyed as fast as they were built. Until we can hold our own skies against air pirates of all kinds, we are victims waiting for the ax to fall."

"Albanian pilots might have greater circumspection next time," Sasha offered, watching the man across from him smile cruelly.

"Now if we can only rout the Bulgarians," he responded. "But you will not move to Belgrade?"

"We would not be safe there," Sasha reminded him. "As you are aware. But we can also get from our base here to New Belgrade in thirty minutes. Not enough time to stop a quick raid, but perhaps we could lure them in sometime and chastise them."

"That would be lovely," Ćosić nodded. "We need a year. Perhaps two. If the weather would improve and our crops not wither, we would be in a better position, though Truman has provided much support and shown a willingness to trade."

"But you prefer not to align with the West?" Sasha confirmed.

"Tito would prefer a much wider neutrality," Ćosić stated. "All the nations being freed from colonialism to rise up as a third block perhaps, beholden to neither side and trading with all. That will also take time. Right now, we need guns. And aircraft. And pilots."

"We will do what we can," Sasha promised. "And perhaps look at your air piracy problems with a keener eye."

"Oh?" Ćosić was suddenly careful and a hint nervous.

"If it is good for the goose, it might also be good for the gander, Ambassador," Sasha offered vaguely.

Ćosić paused, then he smiled.

Sasha shared it. He did not know what he might do just yet, but there were ways to send quiet, private, polite messages. Even with high explosives.

Still, he would let the enemy make the first step. Albanian air piracy over neutral waters didn't count.

But Sasha had a few ideas.

CHAPTER 16

Vanya felt his heart stop beating. Then restart and immediately over-rev.

Graham was facing away from her, so he hadn't seen the woman walk in. Vanya had a lifetime of keeping his emotions deep within, where they did not betray him to others.

Commissar. And before that, other tasks that required a studied, public duplicity.

He had simply never expected to see her again, though Vanya couldn't say exactly when he had crossed that threshold. It had been nearly a decade.

On Sunday, 22 June 1941, Germany had invaded. *Operation Barbarossa*.

On Friday, 27 June, he had been ordered immediately transferred from the NKGB, the People's Commissariat for State Security, to the Soviet army, then later to the Air Forces. Then a Commissar Pilot.

After the war, he had stayed in uniform. Flown experimental aircraft, though not nearly as much as Sasha. Been associated loosely with the GRU, the Military Intelligence branch.

Been in the right place for Colonel Nazarenko to recruit

him when Sasha needed people he could trust. Had probably left the Soviet Union forever. At least if his mission was successful.

When, exactly, had he stopped expecting Dolga Leninova to suddenly walk around a corner and back into his life?

He watched her, wondering what a decade had done to her. Especially the eight—nearly nine—years that had just passed.

Aged her into maturity, from the oh-so-painfully-young woman he had met in 1939. Scrawny, then. Feisty. Unbending. Unstoppable, once she set her mind on a thing, though he had managed to thwart her in at least one thing.

To his eternal regret. Vanya still found himself wondering what her kiss tasted like. She had insinuated. Hinted. Pushed.

But he had been her superior officer. Her teacher. That would have made it wrong, regardless of how everyone else might have handled it. How they might have cast ethics to the wind when a beautiful woman batted her eyes at them.

Vanya had managed to withstand the whirlwind of her personality and the terrible swirl of emotions that had threatened to overwhelm them both.

When had he expected to never see her again?

He started to speak. To call out her name.

Her head gave the slightest shake of negation. Her eyes flickered to his companion and back.

No words were spoken, but they could still communicate with so little, it seemed, even after this long.

He managed his coffee without any of the shivering in his soul making it to his hands.

"Problems?" Graham was asking, watching his eyes and suddenly alert for violence.

Vanya tore his gaze away from the woman by force of will

and returned to the man who might represent Dolga's greatest enemy: a British lordling.

"I thought I saw someone I recognized, but I was mistaken," Vanya lied, feeling bad about it. "A ghost, from long ago and well away from here."

Graham nodded sagely, like a man with his own regrets.

Did Vanya regret? Likely.

When had he assumed they would never speak again? What had remained unsaid then, and would any of it matter today?

He found himself churned up inside, but he maintained the calm facade of the Commissar-Captain.

Dolga watched him without comment. Without a suggestion that they had once known one another. Had come that close to becoming lovers, though he had never so much as held her hand.

One slip would have drowned him forever in those dark eyes.

That might be his regret today, not tasting her kiss once, like the heroic fool in the movies about to go off to war.

What had a decade done to her? Vanya knew what it had done to him.

He contemplated all of his sins for a long moment, then decided that there was far more here than was obvious, for Dolga Leninova, the *Dutiful Daughter of Lenin* as her parents had named her, to be sitting in a cafe in the Free City of Trieste, silently watching him. Precluding a conversation that would have too many witnesses.

His coffee cup empty seemed a sign, though he could not guess which deities—romantic or malign—had their eyes upon him today. Vanya rose and left an American dollar on the table. Far more than two cups of coffee cost, but Sasha had ordered them to be profligate with their funds.

Extravagant, even. Money here today meant that Trieste stood a better chance of recovering tomorrow.

He nodded to the waitress and waved her off when she tried to make change, even as he felt like a kulak as they made their way back into the day. A breeze had arisen. Cold and chill, icy fingers finding flesh to caress.

He would need to get indoors and warm himself by a fire.

If that was possible.

And he needed to warn Sasha.

Which meant that Sasha also needed to know more of the truth about his Commissar.

Things only Gennadi had known until today.

Those secrets might be a problem, if Soviet Foreign Intelligence was here in Trieste, looking for him specifically.

What other troubles lay in wait?

CHAPTER 17

Sasha had mixed coffee with whiskey, an affectation he had learned in Ireland from those comrades. Folks who understood how to mix heat and relaxation on a day that promised...

He withheld his sigh as he considered the nature of the relationship between him and Vanya. Commissar-Captain Ivan Zhidkov. The one Gennadi had originally assumed would be needed to keep the rest in line. To keep them from backsliding, when surrounded by the wealth and decadence of the West in all its glory. It had not ended up being needed, for the most part.

But the coffee was good. And the whiskey. And there was enough coal to keep the building warm.

The chill existed solely in his soul.

The door was closed. Vanya had gone so far as to round up Arkadi and Ilya when he arrived, stationing them outside both door and window to watch. And they spoke entirely in Russian, low, quiet voices that would be hard for microphones to record adequately.

Vanya had looked like a man in need of confession. Sasha had not understood the depth of his friend's sins an hour ago.

"And you are certain that it was your old protege?" Sasha asked as Vanya wound down to nothing like an engine running out of fuel.

"Without doubt, Sasha," Vanya replied glumly. "She recognized me. Sat facing me. Prevented me from telling Graham, at least in that moment, though I presume that all the others will need to know at some point."

"Perhaps," Sasha replied. "Perhaps not."

He liked the flicker of hope that appeared in Vanya's eyes and detested the discomfort that accompanied them.

"You worked with the First Directorate in those days?" Sasha confirmed.

"It was the Main Directorate of State Security for the NKVD at the time, but yes," Vanya acknowledged. "More recently, it became the First Directorate of the People's Commissariat of State Security, then the Ministry of State Security. In 1947, the Committee of Information was formed by merging it and the GRU, military intelligence, but those two are oil and water and I do not see that lasting."

"But you were a spy?"

"And an assassin," Vanya nodded. "And many other things that the Revolution needed in the face of Western hostility and the various invasions to support the Whites and others."

"And you continue to be a loyal citizen," Sasha smiled, watching the man's confusion grow worse before he finally understood and nodded back.

The deepest cover possible, for the longest time, like other agents put in place in foreign cities to watch.

The Red Branch had been forced to act, and perhaps forever moved past their original Nazi hunting mission, though those men were still out there, like ticks in fur, burrowed in where they were hard to dislodge.

Sasha considered the Ratlines that the Catholic Church in Rome had established in order to help war criminals flee to Franco's Spain or to neutral places in South America. The Americans had helped. Or at least actively ignored such things, but they had also rounded up as many German scientists as they could and taken them to America.

And not put any of them in camps to *rehabilitate* them.

"As you say, Sasha," Vanya breathed out heavily.

"You could have said nothing," Sasha reminded him.

"You warned us that Trieste was a city of thieves, spies, and troublemakers," Vanya finally managed a weak smile. "I simply had no idea that they might come looking for me. That my ghosts might be the ones that arose from the grave of yesterday."

"Tell me about this Leninova woman," Sasha ordered his friend, mostly to watch Vanya transform from his usual dour seriousness to almost a hopeless romantic.

"Lyuba's brains," Vanya replied. "Golden Horde, so Siberian bones and color rather than European or Ukrainian. Not a dancer but she could be today, were she of a mind. Grown into herself. Utterly dedicated to the Revolution in those days, raised by true believers. I believe she has a younger sister equally committed, but it has been a decade of war and I might be misremembering."

"But you never...?"

"Never once," Vanya sighed. "Sitting here, talking to you, I wonder if I should have. But I was her superior officer and she was a child. Not a child. Eighteen years old, going on fifty, but still."

"A power imbalance," Sasha noted.

He would have never chased Lyuba for the same reasons, but they were both older. More mature. And he was willing to let her drive things. Both of them were more able to understand where certain lines should be drawn and honored in ways he agreed with Vanya that someone so young and presumably sheltered would be unable to grasp.

"A terrible imbalance," Vanya agreed. "I was her teacher in many things, but that was the one I could never bring myself to do."

"Because it would have been too easy to fall in love with her?" Sasha asked/guessed, watching the man's body language.

"Far too easy," Vanya sighed. "What I cannot guess today is how she feels, because we have not spoken. And unless she has become someone radically different from who she was a decade ago, I would expect Dolga to remain loyal. Perhaps a seasoned MVD agent these days. Perhaps bait dangled in front of me. Perhaps a trap."

"Perhaps another GRU team sent to kill you," Sasha agreed.

They had tried last summer and failed, but that was poor intelligence on their part, because Gennadi had taken great pains to hide all of the truth from any prying eyes in London, Washington, **and** Moscow.

"And yes, that," Vanya sighed. "It might be the perfect trap."

"Make sure Arkadi and the other enlisted men understand that they might be approached next," Sasha ordered. "And let her approach you, understanding that she might be trying to kill you, Vanya. Should I make sure you are never alone outside the base?"

He watched his friend consider it carefully. Watched a decade vanish and things Gennadi called *tradecraft* reassert themselves, from whatever box Vanya had hidden them in previously.

"There will be things that must change," Vanya said. "But I expect her to want to talk to me alone, though I cannot begin to guess which of several traps she might represent. Part of me wonders if she has somehow grown sour on the Revolution after the Stalin years, and desires a way out, seeing in me an avenue she might use. That, or the avenging angel at the other end of that spectrum."

Sasha watched. Pondered. Decided that someone had laid the absolutely perfect trap for his friend, leaving Vanya no way to escape without some sort of potentially lethal confrontation with the woman. Especially if she was as dangerous, as capable, as Vanya suggested.

And being here in Trieste limited his options as much as it expanded them. Pity that he didn't have an easy way to get Gennadi's expertise into play.

Sasha was on his own. Well, he wasn't, but Vanya would need help.

"Be wary until she contacts you again," Sasha ordered. "Have Arkadi and one of the others nearby, but perhaps find a way to be alone in public that your watchers might contact you. She could have come through the door shooting, after all, so let us presume that she wants to talk for now, and nothing more."

Vanya sighed like a man dying, that last bit of air flowing out, before he drew a breath and nodded.

"It will be as you say, Commander," he said sternly, back upright and square again.

Sasha watched him rise and go. Vanya would need help.

Sasha knew where to start.

CHAPTER 18

Sasha finished his explanation and watched *Beau* digest it. Cecil Warwick. Royal Australian Air Force. Pilot. Able and willing to fly just about anything, as he had been in seaplanes and cargo transports since the war ended.

Until he had gotten a telegram from his cousin Molly in Los Angeles about a new flying opportunity.

"Gotcha so far, Commander," *Beau* nodded. "You don't think they'd have tumbled onto who I am yet?"

"Not if you dress as a civilian, *Beau*," Sasha replied. "We don't post pictures about the team or discuss rosters with outsiders, that one big news article when we first came to America notwithstanding. *Banshee* and I are too well known. The woman obviously knows Vanya. I would presume her briefing included Yuri. *Devonshire* was with Vanya when it happened. That leaves you as a wildcard."

Beau laughed.

"Not the first time I've been called that, sir," he replied. "I'll do what I can. What does this do to flight schedules?"

"I'll rotate you and Graham for now, so he's flying primarily with me," Sasha said. "We needed to do that anyway, so it gives them an excuse, if Vanya leaves the base on a day when I'm flying a patrol over Yugoslavia."

"What happens if someone jumps you while we're off-base and can't get to our planes quickly?"

"I run like hell," Sasha grinned. "Two Strix can't take on a squadron of Yaks by ourselves but they also can't keep up with us when we open the engines. Only a MiG can do that, and not even then, because they are not capable of sustained Mach-flight like our owls are."

"Feels wrong, leaving you hanging."

"You'll be on Vanya's wing, *Beau*," Sasha reminded him. "With support there as well. And looking like an American or something, when nobody should know I hired you."

Beau was a skinny, tanned man, with dirty blond hair a bit longer than perhaps regulation in some air forces, but shorter than Lyuba's. Or Yanina's. And an excellent pilot.

Wiry muscles from flying the Beaufighter during the war. Piercing green eyes.

"I got some stuff, but I need a proper civilian coat," *Beau* said after a moment. "Everything back home is a lot warmer, year around."

"I'll send Oleg to get your size and then go shopping," Sasha agreed. "Then you can work on disappearing quietly into a crowd."

"Never done that in m'life, Commander," *Beau* laughed.

"Understood," Sasha grinned. "But if they are looking for someone else, they might miss you entirely."

"Do what I can."

Sasha saw him out and wondered what Soviet Intelligence, the infamous Centre itself in Moscow, was up to.

So far, their overall cover remained intact. Deep cover Nazi hunters. And he knew that the CIA had folks specifically looking for Alois Voss and his Werewolf Legion, with intent to drop the Red Branch on them as soon as they surfaced.

That was part of the reason he had started expanding, however slowly. Get Cecil Warwick and Graham Seabrook-Easton broken in and part of the team, so he could turn back to Lockwood about a couple of USAF pilots that man wanted to recommend.

How big could the Red Branch grow and still be effective?

How many wars would decolonization unleash, especially if Tito's form of neutrality caught on and some of the great powers, on both sides, took exception?

Sasha didn't figure that he would be out of work as a mercenary any time soon, but he didn't like what that had to say about the state of the future.

CHAPTER 19

Dolga understood that others had come to Communism later. As adults, perhaps, having first had to overcome the backwards idiocies of organized religion infected unto them by fearful peasant parents.

It was the sexism that still caused her to consider shooting people occasionally. Even loyal comrades in arms. Mostly because they saw her breasts first and foremost, then assumed that she was incapable of being a dangerous spy.

She studied the man seated across from her. They were in Ljubljana, the capital of Slovenia, for this meeting, a small roadside cafe southwest of town, parallel to the railroad tracks.

Slovenia had always struck her as a backwards place. Farmers, still stuck in some primitive, previous century that had never heard of Marx, let alone read him and understood his promise to the future. OLAF, the only cover name she had been given for the fool seated across from her, looked like a man who wanted to pat her on the head and send her out of the room because the men were talking.

Dolga let that fuel her anger. It kept her warm, because the room was insufficiently heated.

"No," she repeated carefully. Quietly. Angrily. "I do not wish you to attack their base. That is in Trieste, in a zone protected by the Americans. At best, you would anger them sufficiently to alter the balance of power in the region by them deciding to return the favor. Much as their Eighth Air Force did to the Nazis."

Her vehemence finally got through, she thought. Something. OLAF shuddered. More importantly, he shut his mouth and actually listened for once. Small victories.

Dolga understood that her humor had been terrible since first laying eyes on Vanya two days ago. On seeing him in the flesh again after a decade of nursing her rage at his betrayal.

His first one, when he had cowardly fled from her in 1941, without even a word of goodbye. Later, the man had defected, a hardened criminal this time, to read the charges he had been convicted of. A deviationist, which was the highest crime a former Commissar could express.

But she would confront him. In her time. When she was ready.

Dolga would have the truth.

Then she would probably just shoot the son of a bitch.

But first, she had to overcome peasants. Even Romanian Air Force officers.

"Are they really that good?" OLAF asked.

"Ask the Albanians," she growled at the fool. "Those few that survived."

Her superiors had ordered the attack, mostly to establish the battleground early. And to give her an opening. She might have sent more aircraft. Or better pilots.

Or perhaps skipped such foolishness entirely, instead of costing the Albanians a squadron and many trailed pilots in the interim.

That got through.

"But a raid on New Belgrade?" he murmured.

"Tito flirts with the West," she reminded him. "What will it mean to Romania if he changes sides? If American air fleets and armored divisions are just over the border from you? He must be punished. This will draw the Red Branch into battle. Your heavy night-fighters are not as fast, but you have a dozen of them that can pounce on the Red Branch from altitude when they rush to the rescue as your bombers target Tito's palace. Or his military. Did you have any questions about how to conduct your mission?"

Something in her tone finally got through to the man. Perhaps he remembered that she was from Centre, and he was a man who had likely been an ardent Nazi before the coup in 1944 that saw the Romanians flip sides to the Soviet Union.

Thin ice, if she chose to chip away at it.

Dolga was almost angry enough at the man.

Almost.

"Only one," he replied, thoroughly chastened. "When?"

"The second new moon," Dolga ordered. "In the full darkness of midnight. Your first bombs will hit the power station, darkening the city and letting them taste the first hints of fear, before you destroy Tito's aircraft. Then you will go after Tito himself, but I doubt that he will be present. His palace will do. Then you flee, and let the Red Branch chase you into a trap where your old Messerschmidt Bf 110 night-fighters can pounce on them, well away from anyone that can assist."

"It shall be as your order, mistress," he nodded his head.

Dolga put her thin coffee down and rose. The car would at least have heat, and she could get to a train that was comfortable to return to Trieste.

And her destiny.

PART THREE
TWILIGHT

Sasha considered the note that had been delivered by an unnamed courier. An urchin who arrived at the front gate, handed the guard a note, and fled immediately back into the crowds.

The letter had been written in Russian by a neat hand. Given Trieste, that told Sasha many things. One, that it was specifically for him, since Zone A was entirely English and Italian speaking. Two, it was a trap. And Three, someone wanted to both warn him of the trap and make sure he stepped into it.

He flashed back to Vanya's descriptions of the woman and wondered if Dolga Leninova was behind this. Or if she herself had enemies in this town that wanted to see her fall.

What was she after? It had been a week and no contact from her, when Sasha had expected her to reach out to Vanya.

And now? An impending attack on Belgrade? Romanian bombers, striking in the dead of night?

Exactly why the Red Branch had been brought in.

He rose from his desk and exited his office, heading down

to the small workshop Lyuba had claimed for herself, her and Eloise Cutter—back in California—seemingly up to no good.

How many American men would never be able to grasp that both women were accomplished aeronautical engineers? And probably significantly smarter than they were?

In a year, Yuri might have something new to fly. Or the design for what replaced the Owl, because every year since 1943 had seemingly brought a revolution in jet aviation. Not just incremental improvements.

Actual revolutions.

He rapped on the frame of her door and entered, watching her look up in confusion, then smile broadly when she recognized him.

Sasha handed her the letter and took a handy chair as she read.

"It's a trap," she announced, five minutes later.

"Given," he replied. "Thoughts as to how you would go about turning it inside out?"

"Vanya's girlfriend?"

"Prodigy," he countered. "They were never, according to him, even slightly intimate, for all she apparently pushed him to move there."

"Some men cannot be moved," Lyuba noted dryly, then smiled again. "Others can be convinced."

"I don't think it would have taken much more in his case," Sasha smiled. "But for Hitler, perhaps."

They sobered.

"The Romanian Air Force doesn't have shit," she said simply. "Old Nazi kit. Old Soviet planes like the Albanians threw at us."

"Night-fighters?" Sasha asked.

As with everything aeronautical, the woman had an encyclopedia in her head.

"Messerschmidt BF110s," she replied. "Perhaps as many as a dozen. Shorter range radar, so they would need to be guided in to a target."

"Or know where a flight of bombers were so they could lurk above and pounce on someone racing in to stop them?" he asked,

"The Owl can get much higher if they aren't looking up," she smiled cruelly.

"Bombers?" he asked.

"Savoia-Marchetti SM.79B bombers, the design modified down from three engines to only two, with water cooled Junkers Jumo 211Da engines as replacements," she nodded. "Designation IAR JRS-79B1. Light machine guns and a single 20mm cannon. Light bomb load, perhaps fifteen hundred kilograms. Outdated even by standards of the late war, let alone the jet age."

"Sacrificial lambs?" he asked.

"If that," Lyuba turned dark. "Not even kittens, honestly."

"Someone wishes to make sure that Communist Central Europe sees the Red Branch as capitalist stooges and enemies of the revolution," he nodded. "How better than to have us fight everyone and do excessive damage to them?"

"If they are bombing Belgrade, they do not get to claim to be innocents here, Sasha," she reminded him.

"Soviet public relations, I am certain, will forget to mention where they were when we attacked them," he replied. "Still, I have an idea."

"Oh?"

"A misdirection we might lay upon our new comrades," he said, then slowly explained his plan.

CHAPTER 21

Vanya had made it a point to visit that one particular coffee shop three days in a row, with Arkadi, Nikon, and Ilya staying out of sight but close enough to respond to trouble. Oleg Markov, the man of a thousand accents and faces, had dug into his disguise kit and seemed to be having far more fun than the situation warranted, but Vanya was willing to admit that such protectiveness among his teammates was heartwarming.

The life of a Commissar or a Chief Directorate agent was normally one of self-discipline and deprivation, made all the worse when a beautiful, intelligent, **alive** woman walked into it and demanded to disrupt everything.

The Romanian attack was three days away. Tonight was the last night of the waning moon. Vanya wondered at the symbolism as he noted *Beau* in civilian clothing near the bar, enjoying a pastry and some tea while seemingly oblivious to everyone around him. Vanya was the only one in here wearing the bright blue that stood out.

Then she walked in and his breath caught. Threatened to race entirely out of his body, taking most of his soul with it.

Vanya had thought he was prepared. It was a foolish idea.

He held what breath he had and watched her move to a corner and sit, facing him and seemingly alone.

He appeared alone, though she might know he had his own watchers. If her craft was any good, she would presume it. Presumably had watchers of her own.

Vanya avoided glancing at *Beau*. At anything. Merely stared at her and wondered at what a fool he'd been then. Perhaps now, too. It was hard to say.

Golden skin, smooth and healthy. Black hair pulled back. Dark eyes probably bottomless if he got close enough to fall in.

She got coffee and they watched each other across an impossible chasm of four meters and twenty witnesses.

He had laid his own trap. Would she take it?

Time passed. Vanya allowed himself a few moments of pure lust. She would be nearly thirty now. Grown up finally. Become a woman.

Probably a First Directorate agent, assuming she had remained with them.

What had a decade changed?

She rose after a time. Graceful and smooth. Eyed him closely. Nodded ever so slightly.

Walked closer.

Vanya froze, wondering if this was when she shot him, but her eyes held a different promise.

She stumbled as she drew close. Fell against him with the briefest touch that still managed to slip a note into his hand when he automatically caught her.

"So sorry," she said in Slovenian. "Clumsy."

Then she kept walking. Presumably to the rest rooms behind him.

Beau had gone from a simple businessman to a lethal pilot

behind her. He switched back when Vanya glanced over, going back to his pastry.

Vanya had a slip of paper in his hand. He held it in his lap and glanced down.

Ten minutes. The alley.

Nothing more.

Enough.

Dolga had made contact with him at last. And Arkadi and the others would be able to keep him in sight.

Vanya rose and paid, as usual. Glanced at *Beau* without emotion. Turned and made his way slowly to the front door, passing Dolga just emerging from the ladies room and offering her a brief smile that she matched.

Then he was outside, where it was raining today, but weather promised cold, clear air starting tomorrow.

Whatever was coming with the new moon.

CHAPTER 22

Dolga waited the requisite time. Emerged from the cafe and made her way down an extra block, around, and then back, an umbrella keeping her dry from the heavy mist that kept threatening more.

Nobody seemed to be watching, but she was not fooled. Zhidkov had been her first tutor in the dark arts of espionage and assassination. Even a decade as a pilot would not have been enough to forget those skills. No, she had watched him move.

Vanya was still hidden inside that stranger. For a moment, she let herself sigh internally at might-have-been, then crushed it and remembered that he had defected to the West one step ahead of a life in prison. And slaughtered an entire military team sent after the Red Branch in California.

Dolga pasted a smile on her face and walked up to the man.

Like her, a Siberian face, round in the cheeks and sharp along the eyes where the Golden Horde had once held Moscow for centuries after the great Mongol invasions had fragmented.

Unlike most Soviet men, he was tall. 183cm, when so many others were half a head shorter, hardly taller than her.

He had grown heavier. More muscles from the slender man

she remembered as she got close. Calmer, though he had always been tempered and still.

He watched her, silent, as if uncertain as to what to say.

What do you say to someone that you might have been madly in love with, once upon a time?

Dolga held her bile down and pretended to smile at him.

"I wish it could have ended differently," he said abruptly. "That we didn't have to be here, now, like this. I'm sorry."

Dolga had a lifetime of keeping her emotions from betraying her. A decade as a spy and assassin.

He still nearly defeated her so simply. She held on to her rage like a life preserver in rough seas and looked up at the man. Studied him, superimposing her memories, however tainted with time and emotion, over the man he had become.

He took her silence for assent, perhaps. Was it?

"I doubt that luck draws you to Trieste at this moment," he continued. "Is it something to discuss in an alley, or should we retire somewhere else to talk?"

At least his tradecraft had not withered.

"I have a room," Dolga said simply.

He turned and offered her an elbow like a Western gentleman rather than New Soviet Man, but she had spent enough time in this region to understand that the locals did not understand the Twentieth century at all, so she took it and leaned close to the man.

"Close?" he murmured, voice without emotion now.

Two agents, making a public contact after a brush drop. Hiding in the obvious ploy of two lovers retiring to a nearby hotel for an afternoon's affair.

It was a game as old as espionage.

"Two blocks north, one east," she replied.

He nodded and began to walk at a slow, measured pace.

Dolga presumed that he had others of his team watching. She had made an open contact the first time, presuming that the leader of the Red Branch, the criminal Kryvenko known as *Cernunnos*, would have to learn about his lieutenant.

"You look good," he said simply as they walked.

She let her rage insulate her against all the other emotions threatening to buffet her.

"I was surprised that you survived and never contacted me," she offered quietly.

"I had no way to, after the fighting was finished," he replied. "And had been moved to many different bases and missions as part of the Red Air Forces."

"Then you became a criminal," she said simply.

The jolt in his stride would have been missed by anyone not touching him. A flinch of embarrassment, perhaps.

"I could make the case that I was betrayed," he offered. "But that's not why you are here. What happened in the past is in a land that is lost today, and we must instead face the undiscovered country that is the future."

He had never been one to quote Shakespeare, so she put that down to association with Kryvenko, who was known as an intellectual as much as a test pilot.

How had so many previously loyal citizens suddenly been turned into enemies of the state?

They walked in silence. Made it to the hotel where she had taken a room for two days, just so she could meet this man. No doubt, others were maneuvering to watch it and her, but they would be hard pressed to do so in secrecy, and she would have men like Rade watching over them in a quiet game from a dark room.

Dolga unlocked the door and entered. It was a simple place. Bed. Dresser. Table. Desk and chair. Communal bathroom down the hall. Wooden floors. Old paint faded down from moss to hints of dead grass now.

He released her arm as soon as the door closed and stepped back, instead of into her.

For a kiss? After a decade of silence?

What did she want from him? Dolga was uncertain, but kept circling back to his betrayal of the Party. His crimes. His escape into exile.

"How may I be of service, mistress?" he asked, standing perfectly still a meter and a half away from her.

"You claim the State betrayed you?" she asked, wondering what bullshit story he might offer her, after the illustrious Ivan Zhidkov had been found to have feet of clay after all.

"It no longer matters," he shrugged lightly. "I can never go home, so I found a place where my skills could earn me a living. And we can do some good, though I understand that you and yours might not see it as such."

"Mine?" she asked.

"I presume that you might still be connected with Centre," he said, so at least he was no more a fool than she might have guessed. "That you continued doing the things I had begun to train you in, before I was called away."

"And never said goodbye," she growled, unable to help herself.

Or the pure vitriol roaring in her belly.

He surprised her by nodding almost deep enough to be a bow.

"I was ordered to report to a base outside Moscow," he told her. "Literally, handed orders and immediately put in a car to be driven out of the facility where we had been. Then assigned to the Air Forces because the generals understood that they would be rebuilding from scratch with any farm boy or girl that showed any aptitude for flying, regardless of their commitment to socialist ideals. Overnight, I became a Commissar. Later, to earn their respect, I had to fly with them. To beat them as a pilot. And I did. And I survived the war, but had no way of guessing where you might be. Or even if you were still alive. Or wished to see me again."

"And I, you," she replied, still bitter but more in control of herself. "My first surprise after that discovery was that you were a traitor."

A darkness flashed across his face so quickly that she nearly missed it, but Dolga recognized the pain in his eyes.

She had seen it before.

"The undiscovered country," he offered. "Why are you in Trieste, Dolga Leninova?"

That was the man she remembered. Cast in hardened steel and honed down to a killing edge. The voice that haunted her dreams and longings.

It took her a second to catch her breath and take control of the situation again.

"There is a man," she said.

He watched her. Silent. Perhaps wondering if she was speaking of a lover. She had had a few, but none had been able to measure up to the one she had never convinced to take her.

"He is a scientist in Yugoslavia," she continued when Ivan didn't take the bait. "A loyal socialist."

She was proud of herself for not spitting those words in his face.

"Why does that matter to me?" Ivan asked coldly.

A blade, silently drawn in darkness.

"He wishes to escape Tito," she replied, just as cold, just as dark.

A match made in hell.

"And Centre cannot manage?" Ivan asked her, his tones mocking now.

"They watch all the borders closely," Dolga said. "Enemies of the state are sometimes shot by border guards. Look at the recent coup attempt."

He waited. Perhaps he could out-stubborn her. It had been a close thing in the time before.

"The Red Branch could get him out in one of your jets," she said.

Dolga wasn't prepared for his bark of laughter.

"No."

"What?" she demanded.

"You can smuggle him out yourself if you care that much," Ivan said flatly. "I would ask what type of fool you take me for, but that appears to be somewhat obvious, Leninova."

She kept from snapping at him. From biting. Even at his bait.

"So you have truly become one of them?" she sneered instead.

"You mean, after I was chased out of my homeland, one step ahead of a pack of dogs baying for my blood?" he snapped back at her, the first crack in that cool, calm facade she could ever remember. "That I have been stripped of my homeland and forced to rely on a passport from Ireland to travel? To survive? One of them?"

His voice hadn't gotten any louder, but it had grown more intense. More heated.

Fortunately, Dolga had come prepared.

"It does not have to be that way," she purred, watching his eyes.

Surprise. Shrewd disbelief. Darkness.

"If I did this thing for you—and yours—there might be some way to be taken in again?" he asked.

"Not publicly," she shook her head. Only a true fool would believe that. "But if you became my agent…"

"A fitting turnabout," he mused quietly. "That Centre would stop sending assassins after us, but we could still never go home? Forever working for our dinner, but at least without having to look so frequently over our shoulders?"

"Or we could kill you," Dolga said bluntly.

"The Albanians tried that," he replied. "And the GRU. And the Nazis. *Cernunnos* has proven himself to be a far more dangerous foe than anyone ever gives him credit for."

"So I should inform Centre that you reject them out of hand?" Dolga turned blue-steel-cold.

"That is not my call to make, Leninova," he said simply. "I am Red-2. Red-1 and Red Branch Command decide those things. As with you, I am only the messenger here. But I will convey your message to Sasha."

She nearly lashed out when he took another half step back, distancing himself as if he could see her plan to close and perhaps entice him with what he had denied them both a decade ago.

She watched him watch her, then the fool turned and walked to the door.

"That's it?" she hissed. "Walk away? Again? I could not tempt you to stay?"

"There is probably nothing I would like more in the world, Dolga," he said sadly. "Nothing. But it has been many years, and we have turned into strangers. I will speak on your behalf to Sasha. He will no doubt need to inform Red Branch Command and they will make a decision. That will take a few days. Shall I meet you again in the cafe in five days?"

"Five days," she replied, watching him study her for a long moment, then open the door and exit.

The rage was back. Primary. Primal.

Again, he had refused her. Denied her. Perhaps too proud to look back at what they might have had, had the world turned out differently.

At the same time, it wasn't like her offer was expected to turn a man like Ivan Zhidkov. Or the Red Branch. At best, they might allow her to get close enough to destroy all of them.

Assuming they survived the night of the new moon.

The Red Branch might already be gone by then, and she could return to Centre and be rewarded for a job well done.

CHAPTER 23

Sasha listened with an open mind. And the understanding that there were hidden players at work, both here in Zone A as well as just over several borders.

Dancing in darkness. Fortunately, the Red Branch flew night-fighters.

"I agree," Sasha said when Vanya finished. "There is literally no way we could trust such an offering from them. At best, they turn us into triple agents unknowingly, then attempt to burn us later with the Americans and the British when our perfidy is revealed."

They were in his office. Door closed. A debrief, but not from a flying mission.

Or rather, Vanya flying a solo patrol.

Sasha watched his friend's turmoil.

"At the same time, if we refuse her outright, I have no doubts that she is prepared to attempt assassinations," Vanya replied. "Presumably, she has a team here in Trieste, though we lack the resources to investigate."

"And if we ask the Americans for help there, I have no

doubt that such would leak," Sasha acknowledged. "But she gives us time to formulate a reply."

"I spent the entire walk back to base wondering if she expected us to already be destroyed in five days," Vanya offered bleakly. "That the ambush over Belgrade was supposed to hurt us so badly that the Red Branch was functionally ended. In that case, they could recruit the fragments and run us. Perhaps, like General Carlyle, insert their own agents and pilots to build us up again?"

"That is my read," Sasha said. "We are bait. A stalking horse, such as you put out when hunting dangerous cats. But everyone forgets that horses kick. I intend to kick, Vanya."

"And her scientist?" Vanya asked.

"Does he know that Centre is helping him?" Sasha asked. "Or has he been told that Western friends might smuggle him out to freedom, unknowing that he is to be sacrificed as well?"

"Eliminate one of Tito's people, either way?" Vanya pressed.

"Makes us look bad to the Soviet bloc," Sasha agreed. "Or sets us up to become Centre's pawns. And pokes Tito in the eye either way, because I have no doubts that information would immediately be leaked about who did it and how it was done."

"How far do we take the charade?" Vanya asked. "How deep do we go before turning their trap?"

"Is she as good as you suspect?" Sasha asked.

"Probably," Vanya shrugged. "This feels like wheels inside wheels. A complex mechanism grinding on to some foreordained ending point."

"I think not," Sasha smiled. "We have options. And our own tradecraft, if Leninova is unaware of who we really are.

Certainly, she would have approached you differently, had she come from Gennadi's people and been briefed. Hell, in that case, I might seriously consider what she offers. Here, though, she sets us up for a fall. Either next week or next year. She is Centre, and they believe that we have betrayed them."

"And, technically, we have," Vanya grinned. "Enemies of the State. Defenders of Deviationist Yugoslavia from the Orthodoxy of Stalinism. Worse, being paid by the Americans to drive an ideological wedge into loyal communist nations."

"Who just happen to all be heavily occupied by Soviet armies," Sasha reminded him. "Yugoslavia was only able to break free because they were never fully occupied. Tito's doing, and that man might be Stalin's match."

"Do we tell them?" Vanya asked. "Bring them in from the cold?"

"We will circle back and review all this once you understand what carrot and stick she offers after Belgrade," Sasha said simply. "Then we will plan our next mission. We have many more options than most people understand. Keep that in mind."

"I shall," Vanya said, rising and nodding.

He departed at that, and Sasha watched him go. Never in the time he had known Vanya Zhidkov had he seen the man in such turmoil. But then, Sasha had never run into a woman who could so completely turn his head.

Well, that was untrue, but he and Lyuba had at least approached things with hopefully a more mature understanding. And limited themselves to quiet moments stolen here and there.

Was that a mistake? Sasha found that he didn't know, and couldn't offer his friend any better advice.

Especially if the woman also wanted to perhaps kill them all.

He would see what a week brought.

PART FOUR

NIGHTFALL

CHAPTER 24

Yuri had never been a dogfighter. Like Sasha, he had flown aircraft up from Persia during the war, as well as other places. Later, he had flown the Il-2. The *Sturmovik*. The flying tank. A beast designed to engage Nazi armor at low enough altitude that he could yell insults at them personally as he flew by their flaming wrecks. Maybe piss on them, too.

Thus, it had been natural for Colonel Nazarenko to hire him to fly a modified and camouflaged Il-28 medium bomber. A flying command post, of sorts, able to keep up with the Nightvipers and still defend itself. If he had not carried any bombs to date, that was an oversight that might be rectified before this job was done.

Night had long since fallen on Trieste. Yuri looked around and understood that there would be eyes in the darkness outside the base, no doubt watching and ready to send an alert when the Red Branch suddenly took off on a night patrol.

Because the Red Branch flew night-fighters. Even his obstreperous Camel could see in the dark. Shortly, that would matter.

Dmitri finished his walk around. Yuri had already done one, but Dmitri always followed up with his own.

They stood, facing the flight line as the others got ready in the near distance. Oleg was already aboard, but the clear air had a chill bite to it. Yuri felt like St. George's dragon, breathing steam in long gouts.

"I will require bombs," Dmitri announced abruptly.

"For?" Yuri asked.

Normally, his navigator/bombardier was a reserved man. Quiet. A technical genius who could repair anything, though he lacked the formal training and mathematical abilities of *Banshee*. The only other person present as smart as she was, though.

"If they do this, it is functionally a declaration of war," Dmitri replied. "Whatever they attack. Once we have chastened them sufficiently, it will become necessary to slap them back."

"By bombing a base in Romania?" Yuri pressed. "The Soviet bloc news will have a field day with that."

"Yuri, it is not like we can rely on them for the truth," Dmitri admonished. "They will spread whatever lies and innuendo they think will best shape the narrative. As it has always been. I wish to deliver a personal message."

"That being?"

"That attacks on a target defended by the Red Branch will be met with excessive retaliation," Dmitri said crisply. "And that I am a better bombardier than they are. You are a better pilot. I can hit the target I intend, the first time. The Albanians already fear the Commander. Let the Romanians fear me, coming back again on some other dark night to finish the job."

Yuri wasn't used to that level of angry vehemence from the man, but he didn't suppose that Dmitri was wrong, either. It was the nature of the beast that the Soviets and their puppets would push.

Especially as Tito had broken with orthodoxy and proclaimed a new Soviet ideal that had nothing to do with Stalinism. If the Camel was to be the midwife of a third way of doing things, so be it.

"I will ask Sasha," he offered. "Soviet bombs will be difficult to acquire, unless you thought to have Tito's people drive a few trucks over from a friendly depot?"

"I can adapt to American bombs with a few hours work," Dmitri smiled. "Lyuba and I had a long conversation with Kelly at one point, and he provided the equipment I could interchange for different kit."

Yuri had apparently missed that part, but those three were dangerous. Add the new woman designer who was supposedly exploring Junkers design documents and Yuri occasionally worried what the future might bring.

Save that he would be flying it, more likely than not. That made him smile.

Across the way, Sasha waved a hand, indicating that the Owls were all ready for flight. Yuri waved back and began walking towards his smelly beast.

Perhaps they did need to bomb the Romanians at some point.

After all, turnabout was fair play.

CHAPTER 25

Lyuba missed the detonation that preceded engine ignition on the old Nightvipers. That bang and the puff of smoke as the charge started things up. Kelly had found better ways to handle it, and now she merely had to push a button for the rumble of power behind her to come to life.

Welcome to the future.

Twin Armstrong Siddeley Sapphire engines, generating nearly 33kN of thrust each. Adapt the prototype aircraft with lighter alloys than the beast Kelly had first designed, and it was still probably the most durable fighter in the sky. And among the fastest.

It was enough to put a smile on a woman's face.

"All systems nominal," Yanina announced from the back seat.

The Americans were still fools, as far as Lyuba was concerned. Instead of guns, they were moving towards unguided rocket launchers carried under the nose, intended to saturate bombers as the fighter blasted by.

She had watched a few such flights over Edwards, marveling at how incredibly random the rockets flew. How unlikely you were to score any hit on anything, save to park directly above it and salvo everything. And you still had to get lucky.

Similarly, they had convinced themselves that one pilot could handle aircraft, dogfighting, and radar systems simultaneously. Plus, she knew that everyone was currently racing madly to perfect missiles that could track another aircraft, either via short-range radar or infrared sensors. No pilot would be able to add that to the mix and keep flying, so having someone aft handling weapons was likely the wave of the future.

Like her Strix. The Night Owl Demon, come for your soul.

"Red Branch, this is Red-1," Sasha announced on the team line. "All aircraft stand by to taxi."

"This is Red-3," Lyuba replied. "Ready."

It helped, having the entire flight line to themselves. They could taxi right out of the hangars and launch immediately. Spies would still see them, but would quickly lose track of the Red Branch, because nobody around here had radar systems capable of tracking aircraft.

Like other things, that was only a matter of time. Everyone would fill the skies with such things. Eventually, either you would have to fly so high that nobody could intercept you, so low that nobody could locate you, so fast that nobody could catch you, or do something to render yourself invisible to radar. Like that one aircraft from the comic book hero Wonder Woman.

Another woman warrior in a man's world.

Lyuba checked the local time on her dash. It was just under five hundred kilometers from Trieste to Belgrade. They could get there in less than thirty minutes if they opened the throttles. And burned up all their fuel.

Instead, they were launching early, then flying at their most efficient speed for fuel consumption. Assuming the attack was on time, they would arrive and find a quiet spot to hide in the skies overhead. Except that waiting for the bombers to start their run risked too much.

Cernunnos intended a surprise.

Lyuba couldn't wait.

"Red Branch, this is Red-1. All aircraft launch."

CHAPTER 26

Vanya had *Beau* on his wing instead of *Devonshire*. Not quite as good a jet pilot. Better dogfighter by a bit, though both were good enough to fly with the Red Branch. They roared down the flight line, then vaulted into the night sky, all of the Strix first with Yuri coming up behind them, rather than leading like he normally did.

Immediately, the Strix jets turned out to sea, instead of heading in over Slovenia like normal. Watchers might presume some night training. Or a raid on Albania. Something.

They would not be expecting the Red Branch to circle south over the Adriatic, then cut inland over the Vir Sea, running due east and passing north of Sarajevo and then well south of Belgrade, until they turned north again near Pozarevac in the east.

The secret plans suggested aircraft headed southwest from an air base near Timișoara in Romania. Anyone watching for interceptors would naturally be expecting them from the west, on a straight line from Trieste.

Surprise was the intent, because there would be one jet aloft on that vector. Yuri and his Camel. Anyone with radar looking that way would not see the Red Branch, but the Red Branch would be able to see them.

Water below, dark and endless on a moonless night.

"Red-3, we certain about the ceiling on them Jerry birds?" *Beau* asked.

Even aloft, he sounded Australian.

"Affirmative, Red-4," *Banshee* replied. "Estimated flight ceiling right at ten thousand meters. Perhaps a bit less with cold, clear air like tonight."

"Won't say it feels wrong, but it does feel rude," *Beau* announced. "Still, they'll have started it. We're here to end it."

Beau was what you saw. Bluff. Loud. Honest. And a coldly vicious killer when it came time to get serious.

"Red Branch, this is Red-1," Sasha announced. "All aircraft to mission parameters and stand by for radio silence."

This was where things got interesting. People could listen to their chatter. Folks who spoke English could even understand the words. Sasha and *Banshee* had set up a series of coded phrases to obscure things.

The Strix could reach thirteen thousand meters. Roughly forty-three thousand feet as the British would measure it. Well above anything their expected enemies tonight could challenge.

At the same time, nobody down there had radar systems scanning the skies, so watchers would have to be able to spot the five dots moving in loose proximity at that height, identify them, then understand what they saw. All while everyone was quiet.

Time passed. Dark seas calm below. Shoreline on his left made up of several long, skinny rows of islands with a few lights on here and there.

"Red Branch, initiate Phase Two," Sasha announced.

A five count, and everyone came to roughly zero-nine-zero.

Due east. Gospi was the only town of any size between here and Phase Three, flying over farmland, trees, and wilderness that had driven the Nazis to distraction trying to control. And failing.

There would be a few more towns between here and there, but not many. And few watchers.

Faster than Vanya expected, they passed Belgrade, one of the only bright spots in the terrain below. They were cruising. Efficiency over speed, because nobody could be certain of the timing.

The mission might have been scrubbed at the last moment, but the weather was almost as perfect as it could be on a winter night. They might have launched early. Or late more likely.

The Red Branch was geared to move to a spot and wait.

They waited.

"Red Branch, this is Red-5," Yuri called after a time. "Move to Phase Three. Repeat, move to Phase Three now."

Vanya nodded.

Dmitri had spotted both flights of inbound craft, a set of bombers presumably at a lower elevation, making noise, with a team of night-fighters over them, crouched back in the darkness and waiting to suddenly pounce on Red Branch aircraft preparing to intercept the bombers.

Except that they weren't.

CHAPTER 27

Yuri's job was to come at the target from the northwest. A single aircraft, puttering along at a speed that might convince an idle watcher he was propeller-driven.

The Camel could fly much faster and much higher when he needed it to. It might matter soon.

"Dmitri, where are we?" he asked on the intercom.

"That was Novi Sad we just passed on the right," Dmitri replied. "About fifty kilometers northwest of Belgrade. Come to one-one-zero and accelerate a bit. I expect our two target flights to appear at any time."

Yuri did as bidden. Dmitri was commanding this portion of things, watching radar systems as they approached the Romanian border.

"Contact," Dmitri announced after a few minutes. "Two groups confirmed at six and nine thousand meters, headed roughly two-two-zero at three-fifty kph. Time to vector down the cavalry."

"Roger that," Yuri replied. "Red Branch, this is Red-5. Move to Phase Three. Repeat, move to Phase Three now."

The Messerschmidts could not climb above ten thousand

meters, so Yuri intended to stay above twelve thousand for now. Safe. He could always descend like a hawk and pounce on fleeing pigeons if it became necessary, but Sasha and the others needed him as a command post flying overhead at the moment.

"Dmitri, stand by to begin our first orbit," he said on the intercom.

"I have vectors lined up," Dmitri replied. "Oleg, alert me when you see the Red Branch approaching."

The mouse had strayed into the kitchen. Time for the cat.

CHAPTER 28

Vanya turned smoothly with the others, flying in at just below thirteen thousand meters elevation, where they were far above their foes.

"Arkadi, what do you have?" he asked his rear seat expert.

"Confirming two flights," Arkadi replied instantly. "One high and one low, both aimed at Belgrade. Target flying at nine thousand meters."

Exactly as the anonymous spy had told them. Bombers flying low, intending to strike targets in and around the capital. And night-fighters above, all set to pounce on the Red Branch racing to stop them.

Except that they weren't.

"I have them," Vanya noted, seeing marker lights below, moving right to left.

"Red Branch, this is Red-1," Sasha called. "Confirm status."

"Red-2, ready," Vanya replied, listening as the others checked in.

"Red Branch, extinguish all exterior lights," Sasha ordered. "Move to flying in darkness."

Now was when things got tricky. Everyone had radar pointed forward, so they could see other aircraft. And the Messerschmidts would eventually be able to see them, but only after the Strix got close. Without lights, they might be on top of the Romanian aircraft before anyone saw them. Especially if those men were expecting trouble from their right, rather than their left.

"Red Branch. Engage."

Vanya had already worked it out with *Beau* previously. As with the first aerial battle, they would drift to the right and hook inward, while Sasha and *Devonshire* came in from the left.

Banshee, of course, would blast right through the middle of the enemy formation at high speed, trying to identify the leader so she could kill him as she jousted. Yuri was not close enough to engage at present, but could always get involved later if he needed.

Radio silence. Fingers spreading out in three sets.

Normally, one would accelerate here, speed being critically important in a duel. Except that the aircraft below them maxed out at much slower speeds. Plus, they had been cruising at even slower speeds to get into place to attack.

And seemingly unprepared.

"*Beau*, stand by," Vanya called.

"Got your wing, mate."

Vanya nosed over. And dialed back his speed some, to prolong his approach. All five aircraft were diving now, racing down like skiers on a mountain side. The Romanian Messerschmidts had not looked up and back over a shoulder to see what was coming.

Pity. They were over Yugoslav air space. In two attack squadrons. At least fifty kilometers beyond Romanian borders.

Not an accidental incursion. Not tonight.

And those bombers were even lower, but Sasha intended to attack the night-fighters first.

Vanya had the tail of the formation. *Beau* was on his wing. He opened up, a line of yellow fire suddenly connecting the two aircraft briefly as 30mm rounds impacted and detonated.

The BF110 design dated to the beginning of the previous war. And it had been removed from front-line service as a night-fighter as early as 1944 because it was slow, underarmed, and not all that effective even then.

And that had been before jet aircraft armed with heavy cannon.

The rear plane broke apart as he pummeled it. Glancing up and left, three more were burning or in the process of exploding as the Red Branch sounded the horn.

Vanya accelerated and began a soft bank away to make another pass. It was, in many ways, like the war days when fast interceptors chased lumbering bombers, save that the real bombers were even slower.

It was still war. And Vanya intended to bring hell with him.

CHAPTER 29

Lyuba wondered who Sasha would find as her wing, when this mission was complete. Vanya had originally been intended to provide the calm, logical mind to offset Sasha's intuitive genius. She was the woman that brought so much more to the table, but Colonel Nazarenko had understood that, when looking for a veteran of the Night Witches.

She would need someone just as crazy to keep up with her. Sasha could manage it. *Beau*, as well, if they found someone to fly with one of the others. *Beau* as her wing? Two low-level bombing experts as a team?

Cackles threatened but she managed to keep it inside.

The boys had split behind her, slowing some and drifting left and right, leaving her the center. The distraction.

The red cape, waved at the bull to capture his mind, even as a spear got slammed into his side as he went by.

Or as she did.

Banshee howled her defiance at the night, again only in her mind.

Soviet flight training put the commander *there*. Leading

the group and above, where others could glance up from the horizon and track him by his running lights.

Red-3 approached their formation at Mach. Because she could. And it was necessary to flash the cape.

Her spear impaled the flight commander with 30mm fire, then switched to a second that she had lined up when making her run down and in. Because they were night-fighters. Supposed to be experts at flying and fighting in the darkness.

Those aircraft were more than a decade old. Something like ten generations of technological advancement removed from the present. Advancement. And unrelenting in the five years since Berlin had been crushed.

Lamed pigeons, beset by hungry hawks.

Two aircraft on fire, then she blipped her nose up and went by with a boom that might startle cows on the ground.

Mach One in flight. Was there any better feeling? Even taking Sasha to bed only came close, and that was Sasha.

Banshee grinned fiercely and eased back on the throttle, then pulled back on her stick. Most pilots would roll one way or the other and turn back at this point, a rapid reversal to reengage.

She was coming over the top in a blind loop.

Banshee threw in a bit of sideslip and some flare as she came over and pointed at the ground again.

"Yanina, where are they?" she asked.

"Directly below, exactly as you intended," Yanina laughed from the back seat. "Breaking into two groups. Are you bothering them, or continuing down after the bombers?"

Banshee laughed in turn. It was tempting to shoot the rapids, then pounce on the bombers, but there was no way they could escape her, even if they immediately turned and fled, so she sighed and aimed for the larger group of Messerschmidts, still circling around to try to engage the faster Red Branch in outdated aircraft.

A quick count and she saw four fireballs. Then a fifth as she closed. The BF110 had heavy firepower forward, but only a light defensive gun turret for protection. Not even a 12.7mm. Merely a 7.92mm light machine gun.

Again, only marginally useful a decade ago when the war had started. Far less so now, especially as the aircraft weren't all that maneuverable.

Their strength lay in tactics. In a commander issuing sharp, crisp orders to his various squadron members, getting them into proper position to defend or attack.

There might be a reason she'd destroyed him first. Too much time with American pilots at Muroc and Edwards. They took the initiative in things. Soviet pilots were trained to follow.

And they tended to panic when they had nobody telling them what to do.

Banshee accelerated. The 110 had 20mm cannon firing forward. If they could sight on her, they could damage the Strix.

She needed to make them miss.

A group of four was trying to chase after someone. Might be Sasha, from the way he was slowing just enough to tantalize them, while drifting back and forth without pushing his Strix to the material and technological limits.

But it was a red cape, waving enticingly. And the Romanians were mesmerized by it.

Banshee slid left, then raced inward firing short bursts as she crossed their tails. Flames erupted from one, then she was past at twice the speed they could attain.

"Yanina?"

"You might have gotten a second one there," Yanina confirmed. "I see one falling out of formation and starting down, but not in flames. Possibly lost his tail controls."

"We'll look for parachutes later, so we can inform the locals where to arrest them," *Banshee* replied.

Time for more hunting.

CHAPTER 30

Vanya liked having *Beau* on his wing. *Devonshire* was an excellent pilot but tended to stay within the lines when coloring. Like Vanya had always done.

It was liberating, to have someone crazy and good guarding his flank against trouble. It let Vanya push a little. That was a new feeling.

At the same time, he had fallen into yet another new life and had to figure out how to make it work.

Vanya had thought the Red Branch was enough change. He'd been wrong he found, when Dolga walked through the door.

He put her aside for now and concentrated on the aircraft turning to engage him. Several of them, with heavy cannon.

"*Beau*, up and over," he called, pulling the throttle and stick back simultaneously.

A roar vaulted them into the sky, his wingman sidekicking like a chorus line as the Messerschmidts couldn't maneuver fast enough to keep him in their sights.

"*Cernunnos*, I have them distracted," Vanya said.

"Roger that, *Ecne*," Sasha replied. "Prepare to dive and reverse and I will trade you."

Vanya glanced over his left wing and saw a group chasing someone, then two of them fell out of line, one burning and one seemingly falling like a brick as *Banshee* went by.

"*Beau*, now."

Vanya nosed over and went at the other two, forgetting themselves to turn and chase *Banshee* next. He took the left one and *Beau* the right. Flamed connected them, then both 110s shattered under the withering fire.

Marker lights and falling stars. Three aircraft still flying. Nine no longer a threat.

Someone had failed to brief these pilots. Or had set them up to be slaughtered, though he wasn't sure which.

The three survivors were diving. Trying, he presumed, to get to where the combined fire of a dozen bombers might keep the Red Branch at bay.

Unlikely, but at least it showed some initiative, because three of them against five state-of-the-art jets was a killing spree about to happen.

"Red Branch, this is Red-1," *Cernunnos* called. "Activate your marker lights and form up on me."

Vanya located Sasha immediately, then banked over and slid in close on the right, even as *Devonshire* and *Banshee* came up on the left, five aircraft in a goose flight arrowhead, going south for winter.

"Red Branch. Dive."

CHAPTER 31

Sasha waited for everyone to come into formation. One of the reasons he had drilled *Devonshire* and *Beau* so hard was to make sure that they understood the need to come together, then split off again later. Predicting the tides of battle and reacting as fast as they moved, rather than waiting for orders to do something.

Five Strix. Blood-drinking night demons in the shape of owls from terrible mythology. The bird of ill omen that fed on human flesh and blood. Coming for your soul.

It felt wrong, considering that someone had provided exact details on the Romanian attack. Number of aircraft. Vectors. Timing.

Lambs, led to a slaughter. And someone expected that slaughter, because Yuri remained overhead, watching for anyone else suddenly arriving to intervene.

There was so much more than met the eye here, but he had to take things one at a time. Deal with the incursion. Chase the survivors off. Notify the authorities where to located downed pilots.

Then figure out who it was in the shadows tipping him off.

What did they want?

"Red-5, this is *Cernunnos*," he said as everyone started into formation. "Any surprises?"

"Negative, Red-1," Yuri replied. "Clear skies above."

Sasha nodded.

The mystery remained, and would become central tomorrow.

He glanced right and left. Four solid wingmates in position. A dozen antiquated bombers below, already turning away from attacking Belgrade and racing slowly for home. Three lonely escorts, thoroughly chastened by their reception.

Welcome to the Jet Age, comrades.

"Red Branch. Dive."

He nosed over and accelerated. The gunners down there wouldn't be trained to engage someone closing at Mach One. And then he opened fire, concentrating on the Messerschmidts. They were more dangerous, however little.

And had been a trap designed to destroy the Red Branch.

Someone had underestimated him. And whoever their own enemy was that had set things up for tonight.

The Red Branch attacked.

PART FIVE

TOMORROWS

Vanya had returned to the cafe. The Romanians would never forget what had been done to them. Or by whom.

Nor, likely, forgive.

At the same time, none of the Messerschmidts had escaped. And the bomber crews had wisely abandoned their aircraft and parachuted to safety when Sasha had circled back to finish them off.

It had been like the Independence Day celebrations he had watched in California, when rockets and things were launched into the air to explode with light and sound and fury. Bombers exploding because Sasha didn't want them crashing with live bombs.

It had made a pretty sight. And Sasha had already explained enough to Tito's people when they got home to trigger a violent crackdown in response.

All the more reason to stay in Trieste. Not necessarily safe, but safer.

At least until Dolga walked in. As always, she took his breath away.

Vanya wondered if he would reach a point where he got

blasé about that but doubted that was possible. Especially if she was sent from Centre to suborn him. Or destroy the Red Branch.

Instead of a charade, she walked to his table, nodded, and sat as he automatically rose then joined her. The waitress brought coffee.

An outsider—local enough to have paid attention—might presume that well-met strangers a few weeks ago had progressed their affair thus far.

Vanya wasn't certain such an observation would be wrong, but he also wasn't sure what *right* might be.

"Madam," he nodded as they were as alone as they could be with fifteen witnesses, though conversations that had paused at her entry were resuming, if a trifle quieter.

"Hello," she replied with a hint of a stutter.

As if she wasn't sure what to call him. Ivan? Vanya? Commissar? Zhidkov? Traitor?

All of those were accurate. And probably none of them.

"You heard the rumors about the excitement over Belgrade?" she asked after another beat.

"Firsthand," Vanya replied with a faint smile.

The Red Branch was making certain enemies with the air forces of Slavic Central Europe.

Taking sides, as it were, when they had previously been mercenaries for hire.

Still were. But the stakes were so much greater today. At least he thought so. Stopping the Werewolf Legion from bombing America and starting the next world war weren't small.

Or was all this a rising tide of Soviet aggression? A prelude that established just cause for an invasion of Yugoslavia, instead of keeping the peace overhead?

He would need to talk to Sasha about these thoughts, but for now, he had a much more dangerous foe on his hands.

"Then you got my letter?" she asked, eyes flaring for a moment to emphasize things.

Her letter? Why would this woman want to destroy so many Romanian aircraft and crews?

"I did," she replied. "Or rather, Commander Kryvenko did and acted upon it. The intelligence provided was exactingly detailed."

"I have many contacts on the other side of the wall," she said, her voice dropping. "Beyond the new no-man's-land that has come into being."

"So it seems," he replied evenly, voice also dropping like lovers exchanging poetry. "To what purpose?"

"It became necessary to establish my position, Ivan," she said, settling on a semi-formal address. "To inform you of my intentions. To make sure you were paying attention."

As if ignoring Dolga Leninova was possible.

"And you still think that we should assist you with that one task?" he asked.

This was very specifically not the place to say certain things out loud.

"I do," she replied simply. "Have you spoken with the others?"

"I have," he replied. "*Cernunnos* would like to meet you personally, to ask questions. When might that be acceptable?"

"We could walk there now," she offered. "Or another time. The situation across the way grows tense, and we would need to move quickly to accomplish this. Especially as others beyond will be exceptionally agitated at recent events."

Of that, Vanya had no doubts. And he had heard about Dmitri's intention to bomb that base that had sent the planes.

Might be a task for *Banshee* and *Beau*, though, coming in low and fast instead of high, even if the defending aircraft could not reach him up there.

There were always risks in escalation.

How far would things get?

He studied the woman across from him. Her dark beauty. Her bottomless eyes.

He was dressed in his blues, as usual. She wore green, a long skirt and jacket in wool that made her look like a business-woman, if Italy or Slovenia had such things.

Did they? He didn't remember many breaks in their civilizational sexism, but Vanya couldn't say he'd paid much attention.

Still, if she was their source, willing to meet with Sasha, there was no better time than the present.

He finished his coffee. She did the same. He left money as he rose, then offered her an elbow.

Back to base.

And then what?

CHAPTER 33

Dolga concentrated on her mission. On the need to destroy these traitors entirely, lest others somehow think that they could escape the wrath of their Soviet masters.

There is nowhere you could run that Centre could not reach you.

Outside, chill air. Not much breeze. Clear skies.

She had dressed warm and worn comfortable shoes, in case walking a few kilometers became necessary, but Ivan quickly hailed a passing cab. They rode in companionable silence, touching but not lovers.

Never lovers, a regret that still burned. Did he feel it? Did he feel anything?

The Vanya she remembered had been cool and focused. Almost cold.

A match made in hell, she supposed, as she had taught herself to emulate him in so many things and that had provided the template for her later success.

He smiled primly at her, but did not speak. The cab delivered them to the front gate of their base, where armed men watched her closely, but she had come to this meeting unarmed, save for her wits and ruthlessness.

The base was a rough thing. Destroyed buildings that had been leveled and paved to provide a runway. Old offices converted. Cylindrical steel hangars. Newly erected barracks in wood.

All the comforts of an air base. American and British guards everywhere, but that was Trieste and Yugoslavia just over the border, where agents of other controllers worked to sabotage things in order to weaken Tito. To bring him down.

Ivan no longer offered an elbow, once they were no longer public. Merely walked beside her with the occasional glance to track her. Like a pilot and their wingman, she supposed.

More guards. Always armed. Always tracking her. Always professional.

Dolga had considered raiding this base, but the view from inside confirmed her original opinion that it would be suicide to try. Someone had told these men in green that trouble was watching and coming for them, and they waited with loaded weapons and surly smiles.

Ivan escorted her to one building, then inside. Down halls to an office they entered.

Kryvenko was tall. That was her first impression. Most Soviet men were short. Poor nutrition only now being made up. Her Vanya had been taller than most of the people she'd ever known a decade ago. Kryvenko was several centimeters taller yet.

The same black hair as Vanya, but curlier and slicked back. Muscles. Hands like a fencer. Blue eyes.

He rose and studied her like a foe. As she was, but they would have no reason to expect it.

Save that she had come from Centre.

A woman entered a moment later. Tall and blonde and beautifully cold in ways Dolga recognized in herself. Gradskaya. The core of the Red Branch, then.

Ivan closed the door and sat her in a chair while he took the other. Kryvenko sat behind a desk. Gradskaya stood to one side, leaned against the wall.

Dolga had the impression that all three were prepared to move immediately to violence if provoked, but she supposed that she represented the past that continued to hunt them.

That put a smile on her face, though she kept it cool and professional.

Kryvenko scowled at her, but that was unsurprising.

"Why?" he began abruptly.

"Why what?" she countered, assuming hostility that would need to be overcome and assuaged if she intended to get close enough to destroy this group.

"Moscow is already trying to kill us," Kryvenko replied. "Has, twice, in fact, though both were failures met with retaliation that should have convinced someone. Unless it merely confirmed that they needed to up the stakes of the next confrontation. Why do we care what you want? Or should help you?"

"I provided the letter about the Belgrade raid," she offered.

"And we annihilated it," he retorted, hot and angry, while the other two had gone cold.

And annihilated was an acceptable term, from what had been reported. No craft had returned to Romania. Only radio messages that saw the Messerschmidts wiped out, then the bombers understanding that nothing they could do would matter, so all crews had been ordered to abandon, that at least trained personnel might survive, though nobody knew if Tito would trade them home later.

Tomorrow's problem.

"You did," she agreed. "Tito and Stalin have broken, but the two sides continue to talk quietly. Until then, there are certain elements loyal to the Soviet Union that have no wish to end up on an island in the Adriatic at a concentration camp. They must remain silent and live in fear of a midnight knock."

"Something you are no doubt an expert on, from what Captain Zhidkov tells me," Kryvenko said.

So, those two had had that conversation. Vanya had come clean with his new commander about his duties before the war. How did she take advantage of that?

"They watch the borders like hawks," Dolga offered, shifting. "Jovanović was shot, while Kadja and Dapčević were arrested after their failed coup. Many targets are watched from a distance and would end up arrested."

"And the Red Branch can save you?" Kryvenko sneered at her.

"You can get in and out without crossing borders in a car or train," she said, working not to rise to his bait.

She needed them. They had to step into the trap, if they were to be destroyed.

"Who is the person you think can't be rescued any other way?" Kryvenko demanded coldly, whipsawing back and forth on his emotions, but the ledgers marked him as the emotional one. The charismatic leader, offset by Vanya's calmness.

"Damijan Perko," she said. "An expert on jet and rocket engines, currently working from a lab in Zagreb. There are only two ways to get to Trieste on the ground from there. Ljubljana and Rijeka on the coast. The Hungarian border is watched even closer than the Austrian one."

"We are mercenaries these days," the man continued, grinding slowly forward. "What's in it for the Red Branch?"

"If you become my agent, Centre won't be interested in chasing you, Kryvenko," she smiled finally. "In bothering you beyond the usual denunciations. They won't be sending teams after you."

She knew that had struck home as the body language of all three changed. Not warmer, but less cold, perhaps.

"How long can you keep a secret, Leninova?"

Kryvenko leaned forward, both palms flat on the desk and head forward like a magnificent hawk about to tear a strip of meat from her bones.

Dolga paused. He hadn't asked *how well*, but *how long*. As if it was a given that someone would leak. Somewhere. Somehow.

It gave her pause. All three were acting wrong. Like they knew something she didn't, but that wasn't possible.

Was it?

"As long as it needs," she replied, but that sounded weak, even to her.

What did they know?

Kryvenko studied her. Gradskaya, as well. Vanya had gone as cold as a marble statue when she glanced over at him, silent until now.

What did they know?

"You supply us the information we would need in order to plan such a mission," Kryvenko finally said, voice dropped to almost a whisper. "Vanya will be your contact, under the guise of an affair you two are having outside of the base. I will review the material and tell you if it can be done. Then we will consider moving forward. Is that adequate?"

Dolga felt like she'd missed something. Like some critical point had slipped by her when she looked away, but she could not guess what it might be.

Still, the plan was good. As good as she could make it, understanding exactly how Centre and Tito's forces worked, because she had insiders in both places feeding her information regularly.

Perko would be there. The Red Branch would arrive to rescue him.

And she would destroy them all, for all the world to see and provide the Soviet Union all they needed to justify a much harsher crackdown on deviationism. Perhaps to finally occupy Yugoslavia itself and remove Tito and his bandits.

And Dolga Leninova would have her revenge on the man who had left her without so much as a kiss.

"It is adequate," she replied, glancing over at Vanya. "I will provide him the plan, then wait to hear from you, but we must move quickly because forces beyond Yugoslavia are building to a confrontation."

"We will see what we can do," was all he said.

She watched the man nod to Vanya, and they both rose with the dismissal.

As before, he walked beside her, but did not offer contact. Touch. Explanation.

Anything.

Had they finally gotten over what might have been?

Dolga didn't know. Walking out the front gate of the base and hailing a taxi nearby, she felt no more sure than she had going in, save that she had made contact. Had taken Kryvenko's measure and found him a worthy leader of a man such as her Vanya.

It was a pity they were all doomed.

CHAPTER 34

Vanya returned to Sasha's office and closed the door. Ilya was there, acting as team sergeant.

"A few folks that paid more attention than they should have," he was saying as Vanya entered. "Arkadi and Oleg are tracking them back, presumably to her lair. Nobody that appeared to be a threat to Vanya."

"Good," Sasha said. "Keep with it and let the Colonel in charge of base security know to step up his paranoia another notch from here against a potential attack."

"Will do, sir," then Ilya was gone and it was back to the three of them.

Vanya returned to his chair. Lyuba replaced Dolga, at least physically.

"Thoughts?" Sasha asked.

"She doesn't know," Lyuba replied. "Gennadi's work has kept us fully isolated from everyone else. Neither GRU or MGB have any inkling of the truth about the Red Branch."

"We've gone well beyond our original mission," Vanya noted. "You two, especially. But I agree. She thinks the surface is the depth involved."

"Do we trust her?" Sasha asked bluntly.

Vanya surprised himself by laughing.

"Not in the least," Vanya said. "And I can say that as someone who was once madly in love with her. She's up to no good. Dangling respectability in front of us merely confirms what Lyuba said. They think we can be bought."

"Should we play along?" Lyuba asked. "Give them that much? It would involve telling Lockwood and Kelly the truth."

"And General Stoddard, since he is close to the American Joint Chiefs of Staff and connected with both Air Force Intelligence and the CIA," Sasha said. "But only a portion of the truth. And even then, my concern is that they mistake us for double agents."

Vanya laughed with the other two.

"Worse double agents," Sasha corrected himself. "We are hunters after prey that would hide from us. Would hide from anyone Soviet or Israeli. Wisely so. It adds another dimension of potential trouble, if we had to juggle that as well."

"Let us see what she offers," Vanya said. "Obviously, the way she frames it suggests an abandoned air strip somewhere, where we set down in order to pick up a passenger. Except that we do not have space, unless one of the owls flies without their radar officer. Or the Camel."

"Would they suggest we fly this escapee to a Soviet nation?" Lyuba asked. "Or return to Trieste? That's the first mark of betrayal I can see, even before I know anything more."

"Agreed," Sasha said. "We will not land anywhere but Trieste or perhaps Italy."

"What about Austria or Germany?" Vanya asked. "It is less than five hundred kilometers from Zagreb to Munich. We could always confuse folks that way."

"Too much to guess at for now," Sasha said. "We will

presume that she has not penetrated the truth about the Red Branch. That this is all some elaborate trap to set us up, either for a political explosion or her own double-cross."

"What would that look like?" Vanya asked,

"A squadron of MiG-15s with expert pilots," Lyuba replied. "We could outrun them, but would be hard-pressed to fight. If they caught us on the ground, we could be trapped or destroyed, easily enough."

Vanya agreed. If Dolga was set to betray them, that would be the easiest way, as most pilots would be full of themselves after tangling successfully with the Albanians and then the Romanians.

Would Centre commit MiGs to the task?

Certainly, enough people were likely sufficiently angry at this point.

He would wait and see.

CHAPTER 35

Arkadi would have liked to have his new rifle handy to do this. To sit perhaps on a rooftop with a scope and track the men. Too obvious, but still a pity.

Instead, he had Oleg and the new Australian officer known universally as *Beau*. Oleg wore an old suit that needed mending and cleaning, but that helped him disappear. *Beau* was dressed as a stylish American or something. Stood out, but for the wrong reasons, because he didn't look like a watcher.

Arkadi had a spot with a clean view. A newsstand selling papers, books, snacks, and just about anything else one might want. He had refrained from even reading the old Soviet newspapers displayed, however they had gotten here, and focused on other things. He didn't read Italian or Slovenian. His English wasn't that great, but like Russian, he didn't want to be seen standing out, so he had bought a newspaper in Serbo-Croatian that might as well have been Greek for what he could understand of it.

It let him stand nearby and watch, and that was what mattered. No wind. Cool day. Automatically, he adjusted an imaginary scope in his mind for a shot at various ranges as he watched the big Croat man move around, attempting to slyly track Vanya and the woman as they emerged from the front gate and separated.

The Croat had a car. Arkadi had seen it enough times to be able to identify it and had tracked the vehicle to another flat the woman seemed to be using as a base. She got in now and the car drove off. Arkadi got lucky with a bus coming and boarded, staying near the front so he could watch out the front glass.

Three kilometers down, it turned, right where he had been expecting it. Arkadi signaled the driver and departed, walking in its wake and waiting for Oleg or *Beau* to appear.

There. Oleg. Sitting in a sidewalk cafe with a pastry and tea at a table mostly obscured from a driver coming this direction.

Arkadi didn't think highly of the Croat's tradecraft but supposed that they were trying to be a bit obvious. Certainly, the woman was good. The man was trained, but not taking pains.

Arkadi assumed a small team only temporarily inserted for a mission, without contacting any of the locals for assistance.

He had done similar things during the war, slipping behind Nazi lines to do things without letting anyone local know he had arrived.

At least until a shot rang out.

Ilya would be along soon, but Arkadi had sent him to report while they waited on the woman. Followed her.

Arkadi stepped up to Oleg's table and sat. It put his back to the flat in question.

"They parked on this side of the street and went indoors," Oleg said simply. "No appearance of concern on their part. Or playing a role for watchers like me."

"Likely the latter, as they have just come from base," Arkadi replied. "They should presume eyes in the darkness."

A waiter arrived. Coffee. A pastry sounded good. The Commander had given everyone a daily allotment of cash to spend, in various currencies, so they could fit in as needed and vanish when watching.

"Is today the expected escalation?" Oleg asked. "Belgrade was interesting but followed the predicted pattern."

Arkadi considered that.

Patterns were good, but one had to be careful not to start expecting them. That was how one got trapped. Ambushed.

Killed.

What pattern was the woman attempting to weave?

"Is *Beau* close?" Arkadi asked.

"Watching the back from where he could quickly get into my view if needed," Oleg replied.

"Can you two handle surveillance for a few hours?" Arkadi asked. "I need to speak with Vanya and the Commander. I think it is worth watching our friends tonight, after dark, to see what trouble they get themselves into."

"Easily done," Oleg replied. "I have identified several roosts that we can use. Plus two rooftops that might appeal to your needs, depending."

Arkadi smiled. He understood that a professional sniper made the others a little queasy at times. He had had at least twenty-seven confirmed kills during the war. Plus several times that where shots in battle couldn't be tracked down or weren't important enough to confirm.

Vanya might be the only person in the Red Branch who had personally killed more people during the war, as *Banshee* usually conducted low-level terror bombings designed to discomfort the enemy more than score personnel kills.

"Someone will be along and relieve you in a few hours," Arkadi decided. "Probably me, but I will wait to see what our officers decide. You and *Beau* remain safe. If they leave, ignore them and watch the flat instead. Understood?"

"Understood," Oleg replied.

Arkadi settled in and they made small talk for a bit, establishing his local cover and refueling some.

Tonight might be a long night.

CHAPTER 36

Vanya acted as Arkadi's spotter, a team of two designed to slip in, fire a shot, and slip out again later. Alfie, Sasha's new radar operator, had heavy weapons experience. Machine guns, mortars, and rockets, but those weren't as useful in cities.

At least Vanya hoped not.

Night had fallen, and with it, temperatures. Crisp. Especially on the rooftop that the surveillance team had located.

Rather than be directly across and above from Dolga's flat, Arkadi had taken a space one building to the left, and found a corner spot over the alley, where they could still see her window and the building's front door.

Hers was alight. Vanya had brought his good binoculars, but the two of them only had pistols in case of trouble, dressing in dark civilian clothing to hide in whatever crowds might appear.

He was still quite willing to shoot his way out of most situations at this point. Trieste felt like the doorway to some fairy realm, with potentially dangerous strangers coming from all directions.

Other creatures of the night.

Vanya watched shadows on the wall through her open curtain, but Dolga rarely appeared in view.

"Only the one man present?" he asked Arkadi quietly.

"Just him primarily, unless someone has been in there without the lights on. And he will depart soon, unless she is leaving for some late night meeting," Arkadi agreed. "That has been their pattern."

Patterns. Arkadi liked patterns, but wisely never trusted them. And tonight was the sort of night when they might break such a thing.

How, Vanya wasn't sure. He doubted that the man Arkadi referred to as The Big Croat was Dolga's lover. He looked and acted too much like a bulldog. A bodyguard.

Did she have a lover? Anyone?

Vanya had never bothered looking for someone himself, too busy during the war and perhaps too distracted during the ensuing peace and rebuilding. And the Red Branch, with its fame, might attract what some might call groupies, but beyond a random fling, he could not see how he might find joy in that.

Today was like the war years, when there simply wasn't time for a wife. Only occasional lovers, like ships passing in the night. Too frequently moving on, instead of settling down.

Idly, he watched someone pace in that window. Assuming two people, Dolga from the size.

What would it take to find another woman like that?

Were there other women like her in the world?

Vanya had spent a decade on air bases, generally surrounded by other men who occasionally snuck prostitutes onto the premises, but wives were left at home in Moscow. In Sverdlovsk. Or Kazan.

Elsewhere.

Sasha had Lyuba, and those two made it work. Should he be looking?

It was a pity that Dolga intended them mischief. She stepped into view for a long moment and a silent sigh escaped his lips as she looked out that window at the sidewalk below.

Expecting someone? Her behavior matched.

"Arkadi, she appears to be expecting company," Vanya murmured. "At the front door and they have no arrived yet."

"Tracking," Arkadi said automatically, a radar operator tasked with the most complicated job.

Vanya merely had to fly.

Dolga had the look of concern on her face that he recognized. It had been a decade, but some things remained eternal, it seemed. Or she had haunted enough of his dreams lately.

There was always that.

"Possible target," Arkadi said quietly. "Coming from your left."

Vanya swung the glass around and located a man walking with calm deliberation that seemed to stand out. Enough that he agreed with Arkadi and watched closer.

Male. Felt short and somewhat fat, which was unlike most of the population. Dark suit and overcoat. Fedora or Panama hat that obscured most of his features from this elevation.

He moved to the front steps and ascended wearily. Or out of shape. Slow.

Not a man who got a lot of regular exercise.

Vanya looked up again and Dolga had vanished from the window. Was this her meeting?

Hard to say.

"Arkadi, you get to the street immediately," Vanya decided. "I will watch here for a bit and see if I can see anything but will probably join you. I think that he might be worth following."

Arkadi moved in perfect silence and Vanya was alone. He watched, but the window was empty. After a few minutes, the Croat appeared at the window and closed the curtain, which you would want if someone important had just arrived and needed to be hidden from watchers like him.

Vanya nodded to himself and rose, pocketing the lenses and moving to the stairwell that would get him to the street and Arkadi.

It felt like the game was quickening.

CHAPTER 37

Dolga opened the door to PYOTR. No name. Only a codename, like so many of them, where anonymity was necessary for everything. Not her boss, but the man responsible for Centre Operations in Trieste normally, so she answered to him partially and indirectly while she was here, even as Pyotr answered directly to Yegor Morozov in Moscow.

Even here, she only had a name because Vanya knew it. To Pyotr, she was equally anonymous as SOFIA.

Rade moved to a corner of the room. Out of the way as her assistant who would leave with her when this mission was complete.

Pyotr removed his coat and tossed it on the bed while she watched. While Dolga had dressed in the Western style, in order to blend in with the Italian population, Pyotr looked like a Moscow hack.

Off the rack suit, badly fitted or perhaps never tailored at all. Bureaucrat Gray and faded, much like he was. Head as threadbare as his suit, a ring of brown just above his overlarge ears.

Smart, but dumpy.

"And?" he demanded as he turned to scowl grumpily at her.

"I spoke with Kryvenko," Dolga replied. "He is suspicious, as he should be, but willing to listen. I believe we can convince him to act."

"The Romanians are greatly angered, but do not suspect how badly they were set up," Pyotr continued. "It will be necessary to station more units there until they can rebuild their forces sufficiently to recover from their losses."

"As you intended," Dolga reminded the man. "Two squadrons destroyed, necessitating trained replacements. And those men will need jets, so you will have to take them to Moscow, where you can assure their loyalties."

His grumpiness lessened some. That part had been his plan. Break the Romanians to the bit and the saddle, as many of them had been happy Nazis until the coup, when they had just as happily changed sides and flags.

"Had Tito not been able to hire the Red Branch while he rebuilds his own air forces, what might have been possible?" Dolga continued.

Many pilots had defected when the split became official in 1948. Took their aircraft and flew to Romania or Bulgaria. Those men had been trained to be local Soviet supporters. Tito had been bereft, at least until the Americans suggested an interim that even Moscow had been willing to tolerate.

For a time.

For a reason.

"Centre does not wish a full air war over Yugoslavia," he reminded her. "The Albanians and Romanians have suffered terrible losses, entirely as cover for getting close to the Red Branch. They must be turned into double agents or destroyed.

Failing that, so badly discredited that nobody will hire them again."

"The colonial powers will always hold their noses and hire mercenaries," Dolga replied flatly. "Anywhere that they can use someone else without their home populations understanding how badly things might be going for them. Do you think the British will pat their restive colonies on the head and let them go? Or the French and Dutch? They will fight. They will unleash a cruel brutality that might make Stalin himself stop and step back. Do not be fooled. They know no limits in their cravenness."

Dolga stopped and took a breath. She had studied too much recent history as preparation for operations outside the Soviet Union, now that the war had ended. The British, for all their proclamations, had built their colonial empire on a solid racist bedrock, treating natives as third class citizens, and training natives to control the colonies for them, promoting them only to second class.

Those wars, when they finally broke, where they had already broken out, were going to be ugly.

Pyotr studied her, perhaps finally seeing her as something other than a tame women agent to be manipulated, but Dolga understood that she was driven in this situation by a reservoir of as-yet-untapped rage that might be bottomless.

A long pause stretched, but she did not flinch from his gaze. Eventually, he did.

"What happens next?" he asked, voice calmer and more professional.

"I provide them the plans to evacuate Perko," Dolga replied. "None of their aircraft have space to transport a passenger without leaving a crew member behind, which hobbles them some. Once they commit, either to this full moon or likely the next, we make arrangements to meet. I will drive Perko to the rendezvous. While they are on the ground, you will send in the MiGs to destroy them, either on the ground or when they fly up to meet you. They will be greatly outnumbered in the air, and moonlight will aid our pilots."

"Will they fall for it?" he demanded abruptly.

"If they do not, they we have the fallbacks that see Centre agents assassinating them individually," she said. "Centre wishes to see if they can be turned into double agents in place, secretly aiding the cause, before it proscribes them with the ultimate sanction. That is the next step if they will not work with us and Moscow determines that it does not intend to invade Yugoslavia directly."

She fell silent there. They had spoken of such things before. This was Pyotr developing a case of nerves, she suspected, as any trouble she brought down on them would be his to deal with after she returned to Moscow.

Or wherever she had to go next to destroy the Red Branch.

CHAPTER 38

Vanya had joined Arkadi in the alley, a good view affording them the opportunity to watch the man emerge. He was not there long. Fifteen minutes after he arrived, he emerged again.

Immediately Vanya started walking, a block and a half ahead of the man on the opposite side of the street. Oleg had taught him the trick of appearing slightly tipsy when moving. Slower than usual and somewhat deliberate. Exaggerating certain things like gestures.

In the darkness, he was a drunk, making is way home from a neighborhood bar after a few too many. The stranger would be coming up behind him, presumably at a slightly faster pace that would let them intersect in another block or so, there being only minimal automobile traffic about and few folks braving the cold.

Arkadi would emerge from the alley later, trailing. Two men together would draw the eye, but Vanya's job was to distract and let his shooter trail the man. Vanya presumed that he had a car about and had parked it a safe distance from Dolga's flat. Possibly with a driver inside, so he watched and listened for cars with the engines running to provide heat.

There. It was dark but looked to Vanya like a Fiat 1100. The engine was running, but someone had neglected adjusting the carburetor for the cold air. Or the plugs were dirty. Rough idle with a lot of smoke.

And a giveaway.

Vanya moved a little faster. A little smoother. Perhaps the cold air had revived the drunk some, a shock that got him focused on getting home quicker. Something. He did not look back.

Inside the car, a thug driving. No other way to describe the man. Not trained well in his tradecraft, because he was watching the passenger mirrors for the stranger, and only occasionally glancing in Vanya's direction.

Still, Vanya moved without giving himself away. Without staring as he absorbed everything around him. Just as they trained you to in the right schools. The ones he and Dolga had attended.

Presumably the stranger as well, but he had not brought any other graduates with him tonight, though Vanya began paying closer attention to other watchers watching.

How many layers of misdirection and espionage might one find here? Only Berlin probably was worse, since the four former Allies were all crammed into a small space. At least the Airlift had ended without a war breaking out.

What might Trieste face? And how committed were the two sides to negotiating some sort of deal? Could Trieste turn into another Monaco? Another Hong Kong?

What fate awaited the Free City?

Vanya walked, watching for any movement and ready to come up firing as necessary.

The situation remained silent, broken only by his boots

scuffing the sidewalk as he deliberately made noise and tracked what was behind him with his ears.

Past the Fiat with the windows up to keep heat in and fog the windows heavily, Vanya found another alley. A dark mouth beckoning, like a shark's maw in the depths.

He reached inside his coat and drew his Shanxi in one smooth motion, bringing it back down to his side even as he slipped into the darkness, suddenly sidestepping in case someone there was prepared to attack.

He would shoot them dead then deal with the consequences later.

Nobody jumped up and demanded action, so Vanya slid back against the nearer wall, looking both directions and tracking everything with ears.

The stranger made no sound when he walked, but the car door opened then closed loudly, so Vanya leaned out enough to look over and across. Two shadows in the vehicle. Emergency brake dropping. Clutch dropping. Engine revving badly, then chunking once into gear as the Fiat pulled away from the curb and started up the road.

Vanya memorized the plate on the back. Zone A issued, so the Americans would be able to identify it, given a good reason. Zone B might require asking Tito's people, which would raise other questions, probably prematurely.

Soon, though.

Vanya tracked the vehicle out of sight, then out of sound, before he emerged and began walking the other way. Arkadi turned into a side street down a block, so Vanya moved his direction. Base was not that far away, though they might hail a taxi once they got a few blocks away from any other watchers they might have missed.

Sasha needed to know.

Sasha sat in a briefing room and listened to the full team filling in all of today's details. Leninova. The Croat. The Muscovite, based on subtle clues Vanya had picked up.

It added up to something, but he could not be sure what. Not yet, anyway.

Vanya wrote down a license plate number and smiled.

"Will it be stolen?" Sasha asked his team.

He was a pilot and squadron commander. Around the table, he had an exquisite expertise in espionage and sabotage wholly unexpected from a flying circus.

"Doubtful," Vanya replied. "Likely, it belongs to a *Resident* who has been established with good undercover ties to the community. An Italian businessman who was a Red during Mussolini's time, though he is not."

"A neutral," Arkadi spoke up. "No expressed politics if you asked people. Or all of them, depending on circumstances."

Sasha watched Arkadi and Vanya glance at each other and nod in agreement.

Spies.

He did not need to understand such things, merely know that he had the right people.

"Do we unmask him to the Americans?" Ilya asked. "Destroy him?"

But Ilya had spent a great deal of time during the war playing with explosives.

"Or assassinate him?" Nikon offered, himself something of an expert on the topic.

Beau had gotten somewhat used to such conversations, but Graham's eyes were huge as he listened.

Sasha locked eyes with the man, then glanced over to include *Beau* in the conversation. The rest of the Red Branch fell silent and watched.

"I have a personal mission to hunt Nazis," Sasha said bluntly, leaving certain details vague for now. Like when and where it had begun. After all, they had stopped the Werewolf Legion twice before Voss and his men had disappeared.

Sasha doubted that they were gone. Merely rebuilding somewhere.

"We were hired here to help keep a peace, because Tito had access to folks who could understand their point of view, while not being anything more than running dogs of imperialism, to hear Moscow denounce us."

He waited for the Englishman to nod once before proceeding. It took a moment, as Graham felt the weight of the whole room on his shoulders.

"We are mercenaries and might be in a position where the Soviets think they have a hold on us," Sasha continued. "I await the details they propose before committing us to anything. At the same time, we have been attacked repeatedly by the Centre in Moscow and the GRU military intelligence arm. It makes us angry. And anyone threatening us at this point should understand how wary and violently we might react, after Los Angeles."

Another nod from both men. Nervous.

"We are friendly with the Americans, but not necessarily friends," Sasha explained. He'd said this once, but that was when *Beau* and *Devonshire* joined. "Similarly, the British esteem us somewhat, but keep us at arm's length. The Soviets would destroy us, and I presume that this mission they offer is a trap intended to end the Red Branch while possibly embarrassing Tito and the Americans that made it possible."

"How do we walk that wire, Commander?" Graham asked in that west country lilt of his.

"Possibly by unmasking a Soviet resident in deep cover," Sasha replied. "But we would have to do it in such a way that nobody can trace it to us."

"The north is an Anglo-British zone," Graham replied. "Would folks from Zone B ever slip across, if they had intelligence on a Soviet agent in place?"

His smile was bland, but Graham's eyes sparkled with dark mischief.

Sasha matched the smile.

"They might," he replied. "I will speak with the Colonel in charge of our base and then possibly leak certain details to our Yugoslav contact. The rest of you remain wary. Vanya has a schedule for his assignations, and the rest of you will be available to assist in watching, even as we continue to fly daily or nightly patrol missions. I do not think our foes will try anything desperate yet. As long as they think they might recruit us or set up that ambush we expect, they will leave us alone. At the same time, we have enemies, so remain prepared and stay safe."

He watched everyone. Got nods, both from the old timers

and the newcomers. Alfie, *Beau*, and Graham would eventually need to be brought deeper into the conspiracy, but Sasha suspected that they would never need to learn the deepest truths.

At least not until everything exploded in his face.

He still wondered when that day was coming.

CHAPTER 40

Vanya had a meeting arranged. Had arrived at the cafe on time, only to find her already waiting, with a purse hanging on her chair.

Because they were actors, he walked up and smiled at her. Dolga rose as he approached, so he leaned in to kiss her on the cheek, only to have her turn into it and turn it into something...more?

Warm and wet and friendly. And their first-ever kiss.

He fought down his blush as much as possible and stepped back, seating her then himself, even as the waitress delivered fresh coffee.

He studied her. Thirty now, when all his memories were of her at eighteen and nineteen, looking barely sixteen and already sounding fifty.

A decade ago.

The change was amazingly better. Healthy. Comely. Stunning, really.

He smiled.

"What?" she asked.

"I am allowed to recognize and appreciate a beautiful

woman that life tosses up in front of me," Vanya replied, watching her blush now. "You brighten my day merely by being in it."

She lifted her mug and sipped, using it to cover her mouth. Hopefully, she was smiling. It was there in her eyes, but they were both spies in the middle of an operation.

And, truth be told, probably on opposite sides.

For an idle moment as he sipped his own coffee, Vanya wondered if there was any way to turn her, instead of her expecting to turn him and bring the Red Branch along. Or end in a duel to the death.

What would that take? What would it look like?

Could it even be done?

"What are you thinking about?" she asked. "You have gone hard and distant, even as you still smile."

"Dreaming, perhaps," Vanya offered honestly.

He could do that with her. To certain limits. Needed to, as she probably knew him better than anyone except perhaps Sasha and Arkadi.

At least who he had been, once upon a time.

"About?" she asked.

"What might have been," Vanya offered matter-of-factly. "Where you and I might have ended up, had we not been forced apart with no warning and no way for me to communicate with you then. What the intervening decade might have left us otherwise. I have many regrets in life, but you are still near the top."

"Regrets?" She had turned serious.

"Not kissing you then," he said, appreciating that they had just shared their first kiss, however much she had surprised him with it.

And how much was tradecraft, versus real emotion?

They both lived lives in mirrored halls. Could they ever reveal the truth to one another?

Would either of them recognize it if they did?

"It was a decade ago...Vanya," she said, hesitating before calling him that, rather than Ivan or Zhidkov or something else.

"And much has changed, I agree," he said. "Today, we are in the Free City, itself bereft in time and place and uncertain what future might lie ahead. A place where dreams are struggling to be born."

She brought out the poet in him. Surprising, and not surprising.

"Where might things go?" she asked ambiguously.

Tradecraft, or lovers?

Likely both. Possibly neither.

"You return to me a beautiful stranger," Vanya offered. "One I remember, but know so little about today. As I said, I have many regrets."

Something flashed in her eyes. Hurt, perhaps, rather than rage, though the two might be close enough in her case and it was gone almost too quickly to tell.

"What would you change?" she asked, seemingly daring him now.

But he was Commissar-Captain Ivan Zhidkov. The man who had had to fly combat with his squadron in order to be accepted. Who had to be better than any of them to be respected.

To outfly them all, including the Nazis, when it had been necessary.

Nothing in this world would intimidate him. Even her.

"I realized that just now was the first time I ever kissed you," he said simply, dropping his voice down to murmurs unintelligible a table away. "How much I missed. What a fool I'd been then."

"And now?"

"Now?"

He paused in thought. If they were still in tradecraft, it was a trap unspooling before him, but something in her eyes suggested otherwise. Perhaps more. Not **just** a trap, but still an exquisite one.

In the business agents sometimes used honeypots, as they were called. Beautiful women dangled in front of a target, to tempt him into a situation where he could later be blackmailed. Usually women, but occasionally men, depending on need.

Vanya could not think of a better trap to set in front of him.

And yet...

She could not blackmail him. Sasha knew the truth. All of it at this point, as painful and embarrassing as some bits had been to tell. Cathartic, at the same time.

And Vanya didn't think she could turn his head, because she did not understand the man he had had to become when Gennadi found him, betrayed him, then liberated him from a prison cell.

He decided that a gamble might be worth it, if only to see how far she might be prepared to take this charade.

If it was one.

"We have a cover as lovers meeting somewhat openly in this cafe," he replied quietly. "Then occasionally retiring somewhere else, behind closed curtains, in maintaining the misdirection. I would not intrude on your life by suggesting such a thing happen in truth, but you asked my regrets, and not tasting you was one of them. Not kissing you. Not allowing myself that. As I have said before, I am truly sorry I rebuffed you then."

Her gasp was as silent as his sighs, but evident. Dark bottomless eyes filled with wonder, rage, loneliness, and other things as he watched, trusting all of them.

And none.

Tradecraft. And she had been a fantastic student and actress then.

Who was Dolga Leninova today, when she wasn't trying to set him up for a fall?

Vanya wondered if he would ever know.

"Today was one of those where we retired to my room, out of sight of watchers," she finally murmured back. "A document drop. Would you make more of it?"

"Would you allow it?" he countered, watching her struggle with herself.

War with herself.

She licked her lips indecisively. Blinked a few times. Considered how the road in front of them might have suddenly forked in a direction she had not been expecting.

But neither had he.

"I might," she finally managed in a quiet voice utterly at odds with the terrible, professional agent he had known here in Trieste.

Even a decade ago, she had been ramrod straight and intense.

How real was her shyness today?

He sipped his coffee.

"As I said," he murmured. "There are regrets. Things we didn't do. Didn't allow. We are both adults now. I am not your teacher. You are not my student. We could, but that will be your decision. Your agency."

He left it at that and focused on his coffee, already damning himself for letting the conversation reach that state.

What could they make, if they could step outside of their current lives?

And could they ever know?

Vanya watched her struggle.

CHAPTER 41

Dolga had intended to surprise the man with the kiss he had denied her once. Use it as another weapon to distract him.

Had not been expecting him to lean into it. To enjoy it as much as she had.

For her emotions to swirl up and jumble as they stumbled into a conversation on the personal level, when everything prior to now had been strictly professional.

That had been the only way she could contain her rage at things. Could keep it at arm's length. Professional. She was Centre's agent. Their assassin, tasked with getting inside the security surrounding the Red Branch because she had a personal connection they could exploit.

And he was offering her the one thing she had demanded then and coveted since.

Had he found the sole chink in her armor? How many nights had she laid awake, torn and fermenting about him?

And he sat across from her and offered...?

However much she might demand for her mission? However much she might allow herself to take?

For a moment, she was back in Kryvenko's office with the

three inner officers of the Red Branch. That instant when they had all seemed to share some secret that had eluded her briefing officers. And her.

What did they know?

Had she been set up herself? Dangled out there as bait and honeypot, because Moscow had grown tired of her?

Dolga understood that men like Centre usually saw women as nothing but tools. As *things*.

A woman who reached thirty unwed might as well step into the forest and emulate the Baba Yaga, because she was too old to be desired in their eyes.

Desirable.

Except that Vanya desired her. It was there in his eyes, with a wealth of other emotions.

Lust. For her.

When was the last time she met a man who hadn't been intimidated by the real Dolga? Agents she had seduced and betrayed only ever saw the shell, but Vanya knew the woman underneath.

And might be the last man who had not cringed back from her presence, even unconsciously.

What could she have, if she allowed herself?

The mission brief had assumed such a liaison might be necessary, in order to...consummate the later betrayal.

Dolga had resisted until now, perhaps unconsciously understanding that to be a step too far, even for her tradecraft.

Emotions would come into play. Other emotions beyond her original betrayal.

Was it a second betrayal? They could not be together, unless he gave himself over to her as a double agent. A spy.

Vanya had to know that. Had to understand such limitations. It was a perfect inversion of where they had been a decade ago, when she had been beholden to him.

How had it come to this?

One kiss had suddenly taken both of them out of control, seemingly. And she still intended to turn him or destroy him. Or the other way around.

But could she put all those ghosts—all those dreams—to bed, once and for all?

Could the illustrious Commissar Zhidkov subsume himself to a woman? Even one like her?

Was that possible? Was that what he was offering?

Dolga found herself trapped between Scylla and Charybdis. Could she really turn him?

Or would she have to destroy him, once she got close enough to the man she had once loved?

Her coffee mug taunted her with its emptiness.

They could stay for more emotional dancing, or retire to the cover of afternoon lovers meeting secretly.

Was it still a charade? Dolga looked inside herself and suddenly wasn't sure.

And it had suddenly moved to some bizarre endgame where she had to move. Had to decide.

Had to act, because Vanya had offered himself up to her childish fantasies, but only if she was willing to reach out a hand and grasp his.

Was this what hell would taste like?

Dolga rose, feeling almost like a marionette whose strings had tangled. Vanya was there, close enough to catch her but not—quite—touching.

She took just enough of a step to make contact. Let that guide her.

Automatically, she took hold of the bag that contained the

documents for Kryvenko, unwilling to leave them in her flat where they might be stolen with Rade watching this meeting from just down the street. The strap went over her shoulder, even as he took her other arm and tucked it into his elbow.

Dolga stole some of his heat, suddenly chilled to the bone in ways she did not recognize or understand.

But he had offered himself up. Whatever sacrifice she might make of him.

A man standing suddenly and walking out the front door distracted her. One of the locals who had settled in this place, just as she had. Nobody she knew, but an Englishman by accent when he spoke.

Dolga took a step in the man's wake, towards the front of the cafe, Vanya right there.

The air outside was almost a slap in the face, but helped revive her with its briskness.

No words had been spoken in nearly two minutes, but Vanya simply allowed her to lead. To direct.

To control things.

What did she want?

Dolga found that she wasn't sure.

And a decision point was approaching like a waterfall she could hear rumbling ahead.

CHAPTER 42

Arkadi had prepared for such a thing with professional intent, though he had never expected to actually put those plans into play.

Beau had emerged from the cafe and signaled Oleg. Ilya had brought word.

Arkadi had retired to a rooftop spot he had previously identified in darkness, and covered himself with a tarp, slipping behind a small stack of boxes and detritus that shielded him from all sides, while letting him aim his rifle at the woman's window.

Sniper.

His plans had all revolved around darkness, but he had prepared for daylight. Like this, with afternoon drifting down to gloom.

Vanya and the woman had just retired to the flat. There was a light on a nightstand providing enough to see. The curtain was open, but nothing could normally be seen inside the room without one being obvious to anyone inside looking out.

Unless you had built a hunting blind already and slipped into it while others had watched the pair.

Arkadi had been briefed by the Commander about things he needed to know. Who this Leninova was. What she had been. Why she mattered.

His job was to protect Vanya. With a new Winchester Model 70 in .375 H&H Magnum that had been zeroed for two hundred meters.

The window was one hundred and ninety-three meters away. The door to the flat that he could see from here was two hundred and one. Someone bursting through it unexpectedly died first.

His safety was off. Arkadi watched.

Vanya had always struck him as a cold, collected intellectual. They had spoken of such things as pilot and radar operator, and the Colonel had recruited Vanya specifically for the rationality that man had expected the Commander to need for emotional balance.

Their world had turned out much differently.

Arkadi watched Vanya take the woman in his arms and kiss her. There was tenderness, but also immense passion.

Snipers were selected and trained to an almost monastic lifestyle. Everything second to the mission, including emotions. It paired him well with Vanya, both of them preferring long stretches of silence much of the time.

He was seeing another side of the man. The passions buried deep and only allowed to surface today because the woman was a spy sent to destroy them all.

If she could.

Arkadi had already come to grips with the potential need to execute her at some point, if the Commander ordered it. Vanya might not be able to overcome himself in such an instance.

Arkadi watched two lovers explode in fire through his scope and understood that he would take most of this with him to his grave in silence, save to brief the Commander on the barest details.

The woman drove things. Passion, ignited with fuel poured over it. Desire, supposedly a decade old and unrequited.

No, never acted upon. Vanya had shared some of his secrets with Arkadi. Almost as a confessor. A man possessed by sins never confronted.

Arkadi kept watch on the door in the background, rather than give in to his voyeurism as the two began to get serious. It was enough to see two shapes out of focus while he protected Vanya from that damned Croat, wherever he had vanished to. Ilya had not seen him, and the others were scattered around the block now, prepared to intervene if Arkadi summoned them with gunfire.

The Commander had put Arkadi in charge for this reason. That willingness to lethally escalate. The care to withhold the blade.

The lovers made it to the bed, minus clothing. Arkadi had a finger in the trigger well, not touching but ready the moment that door opened.

The confrontation. Or the blackmail. Or the police.

Whoever entered died before Arkadi identified them as anything more than a threat to Vanya.

He wondered if they would steam the windows of that flat, as much pent up emotion as he couldn't help but track through his scope. She seemed as desperate for touch as Vanya was, both of them throwing caution and circumspection to the winds.

It was a good thing Arkadi had prepared himself.

No one challenged the lovers. Or the gods themselves.

Arkadi stood back with Zeus's terrible lightning bolt on one hand, but none required that he smite them.

It was good.

The lovers cuddled under a blanket against the chill that Arkadi ignored, warmed by his own righteousness today.

Time passed.

Night fell, but that one light provided what he needed to protect them.

Passion turned to a tenderness that was as unexpected as it was appropriate.

Vanya had warned them that the woman was dangerous. To them. To the mission. To the Red Branch.

And yet, he saw another side of her, and not just the woman nude.

Not even naked. Merely unclothed. Still possessed of herself and her fire but banked for now.

Much like Vanya's.

Eventually, they rose. Dressed. Kissed, but it lacked those titanic energies.

Arkadi watched her withdraw a small package from her purse and Vanya made it vanish inside his coat.

They moved to the door and kissed again, a parting this time, heavy with promise. It opened and Vanya departed, leaving only the Muscovite spy in Arkadi's gunsight.

He watched her like a hungry, angry hawk. Now would be the moment she would reveal herself.

Whatever mask she had assumed to lure Vanya in, she would release it, now that he had gone and she thought herself alone with her thoughts.

Who was she? Who would she be in that moment?

She moved to the chair. Drew it out and sat, a perfect,

Siberian profile in Arkadi's view. Almost close enough to touch through the scope.

Certainly close enough to execute.

Arkadi waited. Watched.

He was wholly unprepared when the woman began to cry.

CHAPTER 43

Sasha watched Vanya, almost unrecognizable.

The man was smiling. Fortunately, it was just the two of them in his office, *Beau* having been deputized by Ilya and Arkadi to provide the initial briefing, with the others slowly making their way back to base before a night patrol later.

Vanya produced a small packet of papers that Sasha ignored on his desk.

"I gather that your meeting with Leninova went well?" he asked blandly, surprised as hell when Vanya blushed beet red.

"Exceptionally well, Commander," Vanya replied, whipsawing back to formal, but Vanya did that when he got flustered.

"Was it everything you had hoped?" Sasha asked, quieter.

It was not his place, even as a friend, to inquire, but as Commander, it became necessary. Their mission to Yugoslavia might hinge on it. Their future as a company.

Vanya drew a hard breath. The smile didn't go away, but moderated.

"Yes," Vanya said simply. "Everything. Do not take this wrong, Sasha, but if there was any way we could somehow run away together and live in happiness, I would be gone by morning."

"I understand," Sasha replied.

Most of them lived within the confines of the Red Branch, because Yanina had no interest in what she called *The Boys*, and only Sasha occasionally enjoyed time with Lyuba that wasn't widely discussed.

Sasha didn't want to contemplate adding the entire retinue of wives and girlfriends. It might be necessary, for long-term morale, though none of the men or women had anyone they had left behind the Iron Curtain. That had been one of the first recruiting filters Gennadi had chosen.

And they no longer had their initial base in Ireland, those folks having decided that war on their doorstep was unacceptable. Not that Sasha blamed them. And Gennadi had given strong thought to acquiring land in the US somewhere, possibly in California where they had good weather year around and access to several good ports.

Time would tell, but it might be necessary to send Gennadi a message.

"Does she still intend to betray us somehow?" Sasha asked after a long beat of silence.

"Presumably," Vanya replied. "What happened today might be two strangers on a completely different stage from the main action. At least I think so, not knowing her well enough to guess if anything she revealed was the truth."

"Was she that good of an agent, even then?" Sasha asked.

"She was," Vanya nodded. "That was why she got paired with me. Most young women got a much shallower training, because the men in charge used them as honeypots or secretaries, rather than full-power agents in the field."

"Fools."

"Indeed," Vanya agreed. "But remember where we were following the decades of collectivization and the civil war before that. Russia is barely more than a generation removed from peasantry and lords, so old views that calcified minds are only starting to be broken down."

"New Soviet Man," Sasha acknowledged.

That described the Red Branch, because Gennadi had demanded forward thinkers as well. Planners. Achievers, because there was no way to drive someone in a situation like this. They had to be driving themselves, and Sasha's normal job was holding them back with light reins when they wanted to go too fast.

"I have to ask," Sasha said. "If it comes to that, could you kill her?"

The light in Vanya's eyes went dark and hard, though his face hardly changed.

"At this moment, I am not sure, Sasha," he replied. "And I understand the question and the need. Centre might be intending her as a sacrifice. Especially as they cannot actually turn us back. Would the Americans accept if we made some accommodations with our former masters, assuming it didn't compromise us?"

"I cannot ask at the moment," Sasha replied. "It might require that Gennadi come for a briefing and carry the message back to Lockwood and General Stoddard. And doing so now likely alerts our other watchers to potential problems. Anything we do would have to be small and quiet. Can you manage that?"

"I will try, Commander," Vanya offered. "It may be that her demands are too great, but you will have to make that call, because I am extremely emotionally compromised here."

"Not as bad as you think," Sasha corrected him. "You have

handled yourself and the situation well. Simply keep being you."

Vanya nodded at that and rose. Silently, he made his way out, nodding to Arkadi as they passed.

Sasha watched the other man enter and settle, as dark and sober as Vanya had been bright and airy.

Arkadi closed the door and took a moment.

"Here is what I observed, Commander..."

CHAPTER 44

Vanya found himself in the canteen, having a late dinner from a stew pot that the staff had maintained, the Red Branch operating on strange hours and their guard and support forces never sleeping.

Lyuba entered and sat across the table from him without a word, but Vanya wasn't sure he had words at this moment.

Had much of anything.

It had been an emotional day.

She watched him eat.

"Will she ever forgive you?" Lyuba finally asked.

It took him a moment to parse that, such an open-ended question, but Lyuba rarely made frivolous small talk.

"One can hope, but I do not put much stock in it," he finally replied. "Today might have been the end of the chapter that started in 1939. I do not know where the next one takes us."

He wondered if Lyuba had similar regrets. The Night Witches had all been volunteers, aggressive in their patriotism in one of the few ways they had been allowed to serve. And the casualties had been brutal. At least today she had Sasha, though outsiders would probably never see that.

And, looking inside, Vanya found that he wasn't jealous of what those two had. He had spent a decade mourning Dolga, without ever even admitting to himself, so he would allow himself a time to wallow, but it was to be measured in hours like this.

Not even days. There was still a job to do. An ugly task that only he could accomplish.

A necessary thing.

"You just had an idea," Lyuba said simply, still watching.

Vanya didn't think anything had made it to the surface, but who was he to tell? And she was at least as smart—as perceptive—as Dolga. Physically, polar opposites, but mentally and emotionally similar enough.

Extremely dangerous women.

"I did," he admitted. "But I do not know if it can be made to work. Or done in time for what we will need."

"What do you need from me?" she asked.

"I don't know," Vanya said. "Not yet, anyway. Give me tonight to think on it, and we will talk to Sasha after he reviews Dolga's plans for our betrayal."

"That is still a given?" she pressed.

He paused to consider it.

"Yes," Vanya decided. "Whether it remains now, I cannot guess, but those plans were made before today happened, so they represent what she had planned before I allowed things to escalate out of control."

"Not out of control, Vanya," she corrected. "Taken to logical conclusion, perhaps, at least for now. As you said, tomorrow might be something new."

He didn't think he'd said that but could see her inter-pretation.

Would Dolga love him more, or hate him more, after their day?

Possibly both, if they were presented with such an impossible choice as this.

Walking camels through eyes of needles sounded easier. And less painful.

He shrugged. So much was out of his control.

"You still love her, and do not trust her," Lyuba said, taking his breath away. "Will she be there again after this mission ends? Or vanish back into the mists for another decade, to show up on your doorstep when the Red Branch has moved on?"

"Moved on?" he asked, sidetracked.

"We cannot continue doing this when we are in our forties and fifties, Vanya," she grinned. "At some point, Sasha will replace Gennadi as Red Branch Command, and men like *Beau* or Graham will take their place as field commanders. What will you do when you no longer fly combat aircraft?"

Those words hit like a sledgehammer. Vanya had been flying for almost nine years now. It had come to shape his very self-definition.

What would he be like on the morning after?

There was a morning like that coming tomorrow. After finally allowing himself to love Dolga as a person, and not just an ideal and a regret.

What could tomorrow be? And what would life be like after the Red Branch? After so much traveling, and such deca-dence surrounding them, he didn't think he could return to the grayness that marked the Soviet Union these days. Those deprivations would be even worse than were currently eating the British one bite at a time and would likely not end in his lifetime.

However long he lived.

Would he live forever as the traitor cast out of paradise? Likely.

Even if it wasn't the paradise he had been sold in his youth.

"Ask me again when we leave Trieste," he said simply. "I might have an answer for you."

"I will hold you to that, Vanya," she said, abruptly rising with a smile and departing.

But she had pushed the right buttons in his mind. *After Trieste* presumed that Dolga was dealt with satisfactorily.

Whatever outcome resulted.

When he would be free to start dreaming again, something he had apparently forgotten how to do.

There was much to make up for.

CHAPTER 45

Sasha had called the full flying squadron together. Their Irish support folks that had accompanied them to the Free City were excluded, for now, mostly because their jobs involved maintenance and they were focused on keeping all six aircraft flight-ready at all times, against panicked calls from somewhere that someone had decided to cross a border uninvited.

"They have proposed a mission," he told his people simply. "Dates. Times. Locations. Codes. To put it simply, they ask us to adjust a night patrol that slips into northern Yugoslavia and lands at an abandoned air base the Nazis built. There, we will meet with the Soviet agent and a defector who wishes to be exfiltrated to the West aboard one of our jets. On paper, a perfect plan that would fool our employers while allowing us to supposedly curry favor with our old masters in Moscow, who are quite cross at us for being traitors."

He let that land with a dull thump, watching the scowls on faces watching back. They were all volunteers. And *Beau*, Graham, and Alfie were proving their loyalty to the team in all the little things.

"I presume we are not betraying our contract, sir?" *Beau* asked, in a remarkably quiet and polite tone.

"Correct," Sasha said. "Given that we have twice been ambushed, and twice overwhelmed them, I presume this sets us up for a third, where they will bring what they consider to be overwhelming force. The fact that they suggest the next two full moons for rendezvous specifically tells me that they understand the limitations of their current, war-vintage night-fighters. It is a problem everyone has, as only the British currently have jet-powered night-fighters, though the Americans have several new designs coming online over the next several years."

"Someone throwing those new MiGs you folks talk about?" Graham asked. "I didn't think they had radar?"

"They do not," Sasha replied. "But under a full moon, with the meeting as close to midnight as one might get, in a location they can control, lets them pounce on us."

"And we're going to do this anyway?" Yuri asked, skeptical as he should be.

"We are," Sasha said. "That way, we can tell Moscow that we were willing to work with them in certain circumstances, which should reduce the future attacks, at least for a time. And when it fails for reasons that they did not take into account, we are still blameless and the team intact. If the man they ask us to help escape turns out to be a spy instead, we'll deal with that, but once he gets airborne, he loses control over his options, as well."

"We have to kill him later?" Vanya asked.

"Perhaps. Or turn him over to our American friends with the complete story," Sasha smiled cruelly at his team. "They can trade him for one of their own later, if necessary. We will have done the thing, and protected ourselves as best we can."

"But we are walking into the lion's den?" Yuri pressed.

"Some of us," Sasha conceded. "I need to make some extremely quiet contacts on various things, in order to set it all up from our end. Then we will just have to walk into danger. Not like that is something new for all of us."

"What do you need from us, Commander?" Graham asked simply.

"To understand that we have been thrust into a trap by the Soviet Union, and likely have to shoot our way out of it," Sasha replied, taking in all three of the newest among them.

The ones that didn't know the full truth. Might never, but might also be brought fully into that conspiracy after this, because they will have proven themselves.

Or not.

"I'm there," *Beau* replied, still quiet and compact emotionally, in ways so utterly unlike how he normally was.

Graham nodded. Alfie had a look of concern, like he could see the shadows of something, but not make out the details.

But Alfie Ebisu Hirano was a most intelligent man, with a lot of combat experience behind him. Probably smarter than *Beau* or Graham by a significant amount, but Japanese-American and a man that had had to overcome far greater social and legal challenges to accomplish anything in his life, let alone to make it this far.

Sasha studied his new back seat partner. Alfie nodded after a moment, possibly tabling that discussion until later. In private. Where he might learn everything, because he seemed close.

"Everyone will generally remain on your current schedules," Sasha announced. "Understanding that Vanya's operations in town will take precedence on anything you had planned, because they might decide to move early and cause trouble. You will not allow it. Am I clear?"

Arkadi locked eyes with him and nodded once. Zeus, on his mountaintop, possessed of those terrible lightning bolts in one hand, as he himself has described it.

"Everyone take the rest of the day off, but stay on base," Sasha ordered. "There will be another briefing when we get dates nailed down, and we will move to operational status for a combat mission. Dismissed."

Vanya sat next to the Yugoslav representative, in Sasha's office with the door closed. Just the three of them.

Neven Ćosić. A dour bureaucrat in a bad suit, so like so many of them for whom communism had replaced the Orthodox Christianity of their parents. Ćosić was studying him.

"The man is definitely a Soviet Resident," Sasha was saying. "Kuzma Lagunov is the name they know him by, and the Americans are watching him, but not planning to do anything more."

Ćosić turned back to Sasha.

"Soviet?" the man asked as Vanya watched his body language change.

"Indeed," Sasha agreed.

"And connected to this mission you brought me here to brief me about?" Ćosić asked.

They had given him the bare bones. Enough to let Tito's people know what, but not where or when. Not yet. They might try to interfere and blow things up at the wrong moment.

"As near as we can tell," Vanya interrupted, "the team that contacted us is not being run by him, but remains in close contact, using his network to get messages to Moscow without risking agents in Yugoslavia. If she was doing that, we'd supply you with a list of names that you could roll up, as part of our air support contact."

Ćosić flinched. Turned back and studied him again. Vanya matched the cruelty in the man's eyes.

"You two were lovers?" he asked.

"Are," Vanya corrected him. "Previously, only comrades, but that connection put her in place to strike at us. To set us up to embarrass you or ruin our relationship because they do not think that your organization is watertight."

Ćosić growled with his eyes but made no sound. He nodded after a thought.

"I can probably safely brief Comrade Tito himself, but I will impress upon him that you are hunting spies in place," he said. "That should buy time and silence in Belgrade. At least enough. And you do not wish assistance?"

"We do not," Sasha said, turning the conversation back over the desk. "For one, your air force is no better equipped for this sort of mission than the Romanians or Albanians were. That was why you hired us, while you rebuilt things. I do appreciate that Tito wishes to remain as neutral as possible, so I will not suggest that you talk to the Americans about buying their jets, but you will need to do something at some point. We are only a stopgap."

"And Belgrade is trying to mend fences with Moscow," Ćosić noted. "But Stalin is at least as stubborn as Tito, though much older and possibly gone soon enough. Perhaps we will be able to deal with his successor, if things remain contained."

"Contained is our job, Ambassador," Sasha replied. "Even

this mission for Moscow's sake buys you time, because they will want to see it succeed or fail before planning their next move. If we succeed, they may be angry, but hopefully will hold us responsible."

"If this goes as you suggest, Tito will probably have to fire you immediately," Ćosić said. "Are you prepared for that?"

"We are, actually," Sasha said. "Our next meeting is to travel to Italy and talk to the American regional commander who is responsible for Trieste."

"And will you tell him anything more than the pittance you have shared with me?"

"A bit," Sasha allowed. "There are things we must ask of him. Again, the less you know, the less you can be held accountable by Belgrade for our actions later. I wanted you prepared for that moment when you had to obfuscate and be as surprised at everyone else. We are not betraying you, nor Tito. This is a job that hopefully causes Moscow to see us as less of a threat."

"And if they come after you a third time?" Ćosić asked.

"Let them try," Vanya offered. "We are the Red Branch. Let them come to tremble at that name."

Ćosić glared, but saw something he liked, shrugging and smiling wryly after a moment.

"It is good," he pronounced.

Vanya agreed.

The test was still coming, though.

PART SIX
ENDGAME

CHAPTER 47

Gennadi rapped once on the open doorframe and waited outside the room before the woman looked up, glowered at him, relented some, then grinned and pointed to the empty chair next to her immense drafting table, currently flat like a battle map in some command room.

"Gennadi," Eloise Cutter said. "Come. Join me."

Gennadi entered her domain with respectful care, having gotten the sharp edge of her tongue once when he had simply entered uninvited.

Americans did not see women as equal to men, and Cutter had apparently spent her short life fighting everyone for whatever place she intended to carve out for herself. Gennadi didn't really understand her, but he trusted both Kelly and Woody Carlyle when they trusted the woman.

He moved to the chair and sat, pausing only long enough to glance at the stack of documents and blueprints she had been working on this afternoon. All of the confiscated Junkers technical library had been copied and made available to her, along with things from Lockheed, Boeing, de Havilland, and many others from boxes he had had delivered.

It was just as well he hadn't been hired as a spy to steal all this information. The reach of this new CIA and their friends was a bit intimidating, but Gennadi supposed it to be necessary.

"How may I be of service?" Eloise asked, putting her on charming face.

"On the contrary, I am the one here to serve," he countered.

"Oh?" she said warily.

Young enough to be his daughter but possessed of a maturity far beyond her years. She reminded him more of the war veterans he normally worked with, but she had never enlisted, being in university and then graduating and looking for that first step up when Kelly had heard about her through common friends and recruited the woman.

"I have received a message from Sasha," he began. "It was coded in language he and I have had to work out when such messages must pass through many hands before arrival, but he let me know that he expected the full unit to return to base here in no more than eight weeks."

"That's far sooner than expected," Eloise noted, checking a calendar on her table because she always double-checked things before committing.

One of the many things he respected her for.

"Circumstances might demand it," Gennadi offered, without going into depth.

Sasha had been unable to provide much more than that, but he indicated that the mission might be terminated early and the contract fulfilled. Six months sooner than expected, but the Red Branch was quietly being funded by the CIA and others under the table, so they would not have to immediately start looking for their next contract.

"What does that imply for my work?" Eloise asked.

"Likely, a need to brief folks on the progress you have made to date," Gennadi smiled.

"On the one hand, I have spent months digesting all of this material," she said, waving a hand at the various piles, book cases, boxes, and extraneous materials she had accumulated, all locked up at night and guarded when she wasn't present, inside a building with guards, a base with guards, and an American air base just up the road with many, many nervous soldiers.

"Have you reached conclusions?" he asked, keeping things light.

Gennadi flew aircraft. He did not design them. That was what he had Lyuba for, and now Kelly and Eloise.

"The Germans could have revolutionized air travel and air combat, had the Eighth Air Force not crippled their infrastructure," Eloise noted professorially. "They had jets that were much better than any piston driven aircraft in the sky, but not in sufficient numbers to tip the scales back in their favor. From these other notes that someone acquired, the Soviet Air Forces successfully built their OKB-1 EF 131 as a copy of the JU-287, but never followed through with it. Instead, they immediately moved on to the OKB-1 140 Fast Reconnaissance Bomber design, but have not made much progress, for reasons that are not at all obvious."

"A suggestion?" he asked, waiting for her to nod compactly. "Someone in Moscow was probably threatened by the success of the new design, and twisted a few key minds into delaying things, or sabotaging tests. The great men who lead the most famous design bureaus are a bunch of touchy, old hens, forever pecking at one another, to the detriment of the Union itself."

"And you were close enough to witness this?" she asked, penetratingly.

But the woman had already struck him as being too damned smart for her own good. Or his. At some point, she would have to learn the whole truth, if she hadn't figured it out on her own by then.

That fear kept him awake at night.

"I was," he said. "As a bureaucrat, seated along the outer wall and taking notes during some of those meetings, when they devolved into screaming matches that were never reflected in the notes."

"Oh, but they were," Eloise grinned, pulling out a stack. "One merely has to grasp what the phrase 'disagreements were noted, but not resolved,' means from an academic point of view. Yes, they could not move forward. Might give up entirely on the forward-swept design, because it is so complex."

"But you have made progress?" he asked, observing the woman's technical genius come to the fore. Another one like Gradskaya. Frightening, really, how smart those two women might be.

"I have," Eloise replied. "The wing warping is a dual factor. Poor materials in the design, and poor understanding of how to adjust for it. I have four rough designs in mind, but they will take time to create the necessary technical drawings and do the math to determine which should be taken to the windtunnel model stage."

Gennadi blinked, shocked almost out of his wits.

Already?

Her smile was knowing. And predatory. Hopefully, he wasn't prey today.

"What do you need?" he asked, mouth gone dry and choking.

"A design bureau like your people in Moscow had," she replied. "I understand that Kelly Johnson has his special team doing such things, but was not sure if your new masters would allow that much lateral communication, given the nature of the materials at hand."

"Meaning?"

"Meaning, does the US Government have that much faith in Lockheed's special department that I should ask them to help? Or should I be talking to you about hiring a team of drafters and mathematicians to handle things entirely within the Red Branch?"

"What do you need?" he asked, cursing that he sounded like a broken record skipping. "What would a design bureau look like in your mind?"

Gennadi was quite familiar with such things from Moscow.

The many OKBs. Опытно-Конструкторское Бюро. Experimental Design Bureaus.

The GRU was always listening in on their operations, studying what they were doing as they dealt with espionage games to steal information and stop thieves.

"Aeronautical engineers," Eloise said, ticking her fingers as she spoke. "Drafters, and there are many women exceptional at such things. Mathematicians, or engineers who could build one of these new electrical computing devices I have heard about. Those will replace computers, which is generally a term for a woman doing advanced mathematical work."

Gennadi nodded.

"What changes if you are not needing to scale beyond this team?" he hedged.

"Then we are firmly in the realm of experimental proto-types," she nodded. "A bit more fragile because we will not be building enough of them to stabilize on a single, mass-produced design that works out every possible kink, but also things where we could iterate quickly. Perhaps putting Red-5 in a new large aircraft every year, as he did flight testing that might be sent back to Kelly or the CIA for broader dissemination."

Yes, this woman understood intelligence security. Quite well, in fact. And could keep secrets, or she would never be here. Even Chuck, for all his discipline records during the war, had admitted that boredom, more than anything, had been his major difficulty. Give him a task with authority and strict boundaries wide enough for his artist's soul to color in, and he could probably sell snow to Karelians profitably.

Anything, really.

Like, setting up and managing the business side of an aeronautical design bureau?

"What about the Strix?" Gennadi asked, wondering how dangerous this woman was.

"The XF-90 was a poor design," she replied. "Kelly overdid things because nobody understood Mach-flight well enough at that point. The new F-90B that the Red Branch flies is much lighter, without sacrificing much sturdiness. The British make better engines for now, but that will likely change over the next several years. I would put Red-5 in a new bomber and let him fly it hard, before putting the team in forward-swept fighters. At least for now."

"For now?"

He watched her turn and locate a different folder.

"Grumman is working on a swept-wing fighter, where the wings pivot back for speed and forward for stability and control when landing, which an aggressive rear sweep makes difficult," she said. "The tests on the XF10F look interesting, but I think you will need automated electronic controls managing things to make it really work. The forward sweep gives you speed without sacrificing control on landing. It is, however, a much harder task to solve."

"But you have?" he asked.

She nodded. Grinned triumphantly.

"Four designs to draw and calculate," she said. "That would take me at least a year by myself. Then I can tell you which one to have Kelly or someone else build."

Gennadi remembered to breathe, having forgotten at some point.

"Let me contact Woody," he managed. "I will get you resources."

That was a promise he could make.

He didn't tell her that Sasha had suggested either more Moscow troubles, or the possibility of peace with those folks. Either way, he was deep cover. Long term.

A Nazi hunter and not a spy intending to relay every technical or military secret he uncovered back to Moscow.

Let them earn their own rubles.

"But Lyuba might be here in two months?" Eloise asked. "I would like to show her and get her opinion, since she has the most expertise at low-level, slow-speed operations. She was one of the Night Witches, after all."

"I will keep you updated," Gennadi said, rising, perhaps only slightly scared.

What might this woman invent for them?

CHAPTER 48

Vanya smiled when she entered the cafe. Sighed, but only to himself.

Oleg watched from nearby. *Beau* was elsewhere. Arkadi had a team outside, ready for massive violence as necessary.

It had been a week. She matched his smile, but Vanya could see the brittleness underneath it.

Not bitter, he didn't think, but uncertain.

Hopefully, merely a crisis of conscience, and not a decision that she had made a terrible mistake and needed to rectify it by killing him.

But he would deal with that if it came.

He rose. Kissed her lightly on the cheek. Noted her faintest, controlled flinch. Sat her and then retook his space.

"You look well," he said simply.

Some of the frost melted in her eyes, but not much. Not enough.

"Thank you," she replied quietly. "You, as well."

Coffee came. They sipped. Made small talk of little consequence.

Two lovers, meeting in daylight. In public.

Not in secrecy, because so many meetings had started here before withdrawing...elsewhere.

"There is news," he offered as she got one mug of warmth inside her. Hopefully it would help "Should we retire to discuss it?"

There. Another flinch. Vanya wasn't sure what they presaged, but her tradecraft was not up to the day, that much was obvious.

Arkadi had offered hints but been unable to know anything for certain. Only images. Those images suggested a woman under great emotional turmoil.

Vanya still didn't know where she would land when she finally jumped.

"Yes," she said primly, after a pause almost unnoticeable.

Almost.

He rose. Took her arm. Felt a single shiver that she suppressed. Nodded. Walked.

The day had turned unseasonably warm, a front coming through and brightening things for the Free City, though the mountains were likely having mud and avalanches.

Vanya led her out onto the sidewalk, then let her turn him in the direction of the flat she had kept for rendezvous. He walked slowly, uncertain as she was giving off conflicting signals.

At least she was unlikely to be paying that close attention, as they walked right by *Beau*, on the sidewalk of a cafe. Or Nihon, buying a pastry.

Vanya felt protected.

"Are you okay?" he murmured to her, causing Dolga's head to rotate like an owls. "You seem off."

She absorbed that in silence. He slowed their pace but kept walking.

It was doubtful that they would have another afternoon like last time. At least today. But he also didn't want to say or imply any rejection of the woman when she felt fragile.

Still, it was as though a stranger had taken her place.

"What news?" she finally asked.

"Commander Kryvenko believes that we can make the mission a success," Vanya told her. "He wished me to convey that to you, so that you had time to adequately prepare yourself and your charge. I have a note with some details to pass along. Tweaks and minor adjustments, but nothing that changes the overall shape."

"You will go through with it?" she asked, voice unconvinced.

Uncertain.

"As you have said previously, the Red Branch are considered traitors in Moscow, while we see ourselves as unprovoked exiles," he said. "Our hope is that we can reach an accommodation with your superiors that allows us to continue to survive in the West, since we cannot ever return home."

"Your new masters would allow such a thing?" she pressed, some fire finally coming into her eyes as they ambled along a sidewalk filled with bustling people enjoying the glorious day.

"They merely employ us," Vanya replied. "In this instance, they saw us as a usefully neutral third party that might step in while the various great powers stayed on the sidelines for the most part. At some point, they have mentioned a need to hunt the Werewolf Legion down and crush it utterly, so I expect that to become a mission after this."

There. Dolga Leninova finally appeared. Hard. Deadly. Certain. Something that had been missing before now.

"So you do not belong to either side?" she asked, changing mental tack.

"Your masters cast us out," he reminded her. "Hung death sentences on some, and decades of hard, Siberian labor on the others. What would you have done?"

He did not necessarily regret the angry passion such talk arose but contained it to just the two of them as they walked.

She subsided some. Shrugged in such a way that she leaned into him a bit.

"You are in an impossible situation," she breathed. "And I put you there."

"No," he said, watching her head snap around. "You might be their agent in this, but *they* put us there. Sasha does not hold you accountable. Nor do I."

"Truly?" she asked, dark eyes somehow turning bright for a moment.

Surprise. Regret. Longing?

"Truly," he said. "You are doing what you believe is right. I would expect no less of you. Grant me equal agency to do the same."

Another shiver passed through her like a wave passing under a small boat, lifting it and setting it back down without damaging anything in the motion.

She studied him, turning inward until they stopped in the middle of the sidewalk and folks had to brush around like salmon spawning. Some internal conversation never even made it to her eyes, except as a flare that subsided. Then Dolga came to some decision.

"Come," she said, turning and drawing him into motion again. Toward the steps. "We will not have many more opportunities."

Vanya followed, questions on his lips unasked.

Perhaps never asked.

Her stride lengthened as they moved, her flat drawing closer with each step. Arkadi would be silently watching, ready to intervene, but Vanya did not think she had violence in mind.

Only betrayal.

CHAPTER 49

Sasha stepped back from the Ambassador's car as the man closed the door.

"You are certain?" Ćosić asked as the driver up front started the engine.

"I am not, sir," Sasha replied. "However, our charade must be played out in this manner, if it is to work. Thank you for understanding, and I promise that we will tell you more, when it comes time to provide official documentation."

Ćosić shrugged.

"I cannot imagine a more dangerous way to conclude this situation, Kryvenko," he said. "But we have moved past that point. I wish you luck in this endeavor. And future ones, if you are suddenly my foe tomorrow."

"Never your foe by choice, Ambassador," Sasha replied. "Circumstances may demand it, but that will be a different thing. And thank you for your help in this."

Ćosić shook his head and shrugged.

"Driver, go."

Sasha watched his car accelerate and turn away to the main gate, then turned himself inward and ascended the steps, retracing his way to the briefing room, where he found most of the team present and waiting.

He looked at his watch and did the necessary calculations, then took a seat at the big conference room table and drew a heavy breath.

"It has begun," he said. "Ambassador Ćosić will cross the border and deliver our package. Tomorrow night, we will fly."

"Everything has been approved?" Graham asked.

Unconvinced, but he wasn't privy to the sorts of contacts that Sasha could invoke if he found it necessary. And General Stoddard had insisted on certain preparations before they left California.

Sasha had simply never expected to invoke them.

Until Dolga Leninova forced his hand.

"It has," Sasha acknowledged. "Everyone is confined to base and the gates will be closed to all visitors now that the Ambassador has departed."

"Cattle in the chute," Yuri muttered.

"You are not wrong, old friend," Sasha agreed. "And I wish it did not come to this, but the Red Branch will not be intimidated. Nor threatened. Not without terrible consequences raining down upon someone's head. Everyone make peace with yourselves tonight, then stay up late and sleep in tomorrow. After lunch, there will be naps, as we will be flying a night mission to Zagreb for a midnight rendezvous. Dismissed."

Quickly, he was alone, save for Vanya, still sitting quietly.

"At least I had a final meal for the condemned man," Vanya mused darkly. "Even better than the first, though that might have been the finality of the thing."

"At least you had that chance," Sasha agreed with him. "When we get home, we will need to see about how we can make space for everyone to consider relationships and attachments to civilians. That will include you, Vanya."

"I will not dispute you today, Sasha," the man shrugged. "But I will also not believe you yet, either."

"Fair," Sasha allowed. "She will be something that takes time to get over. Hopefully, not another decade."

"No, I will not allow myself that long," Vanya nodded. "Perhaps two days flight back to California when it is done. How quickly will Tito fire us and demand our withdrawal?"

"Once the truth comes out?" Sasha asked. "At least the truth as it will be spun in the halls of power? Not long. They will have to save face, but Ambassador Ćosić knows the truth of things and will quietly whisper it in the right ears. If this goes as I expect, their anger will be a perfunctory thing."

"Assuming we survive," Vanya noted.

"Aye," Sasha agreed. "Assuming we survive."

They still had to manage that, against whatever final betrayal Leninova had for them.

Because Sasha had no doubts on that.

CHAPTER 50

Earlier, Vanya had watched the sun set. Now, a moonlit night had fallen completely. Symbolic, but he hoped that even that much was limited.

All things considered, though, it was an ending. A time of closure.

At least, as Sasha had noted, he had gotten that much. The ability to finally acknowledge his love for the woman. And to torture himself, however briefly, with might-have-beens.

Tomorrow, he had no doubts, they would be mortal enemies again. Assuming they both survived this stupidity.

Yuri walked close as Vanya finished walking around his aircraft and inspecting it. Vanya would be the one carrying this Yugoslav scientist to freedom, so Arkadi was not with him. It left a hole in things that Vanya had not been prepared to face.

"How are you holding up?" Yuri asked.

Vanya paused and asked himself that same question.

"It will be hard, but necessary," Vanya replied grimly.

"She might not betray you," Yuri offered. "Us."

"And I, as the Americans might say, have a bridge in Brooklyn that I could sell you, cheap," Vanya replied, eliciting a forced chuckle from both of them. "I have no expectations here."

"No, but you had the opportunities to revisit your old ghosts and put some of them to rest," Yuri pointed out.

"That I have," Vanya acknowledged. "While generating new ones, no doubt."

"No doubt, indeed," Yuri shrugged. "And I am sorry that we could not land with you when it comes time. But there will be too much going on."

"Indeed," Vanya nodded. "But we have done as much as we can to mitigate circumstances and prepare for what is coming."

"Dmitri would still like to take a trip to Romania and offer a raised finger to certain individuals," Yuri laughed. "As it is, they might escape his wrath, your needs being greater."

"I will have a talk with Sasha about possibly doing something later," Vanya replied. "Perhaps we could fly to Austria in a private cargo plane, such as flown by our friend Chao Yan Ni and her husband Reuben. I think they would appreciate whatever practical joke we might initiate."

"One of these days, I have considered the need for a heavy bomber," Yuri said quietly. "A true flying command post, though I doubt that any jet version would have the necessary endurance to handle such a task, just as propellers lack the speed to keep up with the Red Branch."

"Perhaps the North American F-82 Twin Mustang could be a template?" Vanya asked. "Two Camels?"

"Likely, someone will need to put turbojets on one of those B-50 bombers and see what can be done. Their current aircraft are all intended as long-range, high-altitude, insertion bombers, outrunning defenders and flying too high to be engaged. I probably don't need that much speed, but the ability to carry several spare passengers would save you this difficulty."

"It is my responsibility," Vanya replied. "She was my contact. My student. Now, my lover. I will deal with her."

"Just remember that the rest of us are flying nearby, prepared to help," Yuri said, nodding, then moving back towards the Camel.

Yuri was their flying command post tonight. And had added extra fuel bladders in the bomb bay, plumbed to handle aerial refueling of the rest of the team as needed. Plus everyone was carrying external fuel tanks that could be jettisoned in an emergency.

Because Sasha assumed trouble, and thoroughly prepared everyone for what form it might take.

Beyond a short, voluptuous Siberian woman with bottomless eyes.

Vanya nodded to his ground crew and climbed the ladder to the cockpit.

This was going to be a long night.

Or a short one.

CHAPTER 51

Sasha enjoyed the night sky.

Not a single cloud, anywhere to be seen. Full moon shining down like a spotlight illuminating the scene on a stage.

And it was. Shakespeare had warned them, but few had listened to the man.

And every one of them had a part to play, though his was to stand in the wings tonight. At least for a time.

"Red Branch, this is Red-1," he said on the team radio. "Stand by for a long patrol orbit over our target."

Five owls, like geese, an arrowhead piercing the darkness. The F-90B, upgraded as the Strix night-fighter. Out at the cutting edge of technology, because Lyuba had saved the world by flying the silver eagle to safety and introducing all of them to the right Americans.

To Lockwood. To Kelly. Even to General Stoddard.

The future that was still being born, even as two titans scowled mightily at one another from corners in the fighting ring.

Behind them, the Free City. Trieste, which might yet turn into another Monaco, if enough people would allow it. Ahead, a new Yugoslavia, still struggling to be born, even a generation later, just like the Soviet Union.

A proud people, willing to push back on external domination. And fight for their dreams.

Anti-colonialism wasn't always limited to the vast empires of the British or the French.

Or even the Americans, though Sasha suspected that those wars would take much longer to play out. Especially if the Soviet Union got directly involved in meddling.

And tonight, the Red Branch would be playing a role that likely caused yet more mischief. Or an outright war. The dawn would tell him.

"Beginning turn now," Sasha announced, banking onto his right wing softly.

Below them, in the close southern distance, Zagreb. They were flying high for the moment, merely inspecting things with their radar systems.

Overhead, Yuri and Dmitri would be doing the same, but staying separate, where they could point their radars at distant Romania and keep watch for impending trouble.

It might come from anywhere, but better to be prepared and he suspected that Romania would be the origin.

Much as he hoped that it would not be necessary to confront.

Sasha did not have much faith on this topic.

Or rather, it was all bad, but he understood many of the players. Perhaps not by name, but certainly by type.

"Red-5, any news?" he asked vaguely as they completed the first half of that wide, arcing turn to explore the Yugoslav night sky.

"Negative, Red-1," Dmitri replied. "Staying sharp at this end."

Sasha nodded. They continued their patrol.

Eventually, they returned to that starting point in their orbit, flying high and slow and making sure.

Because tonight, he had to be sure.

"Red Branch, this is Red-1," he announced sternly. "Red-2, begin your descent."

CHAPTER 52

Vanya nodded and broke out of the formation by tipping his nose over and cutting the throttle. Most of Yugoslavia was dark at night, with Zagreb some twenty-five kilometers away, over a low rise of hills.

The space back towards Trieste was largely hills and black forest, with only long valleys providing roads to the coast from here. It had bottled up the Germans terribly at the time, forcing them to commit far more divisions of troops than anyone had expected for this area.

Thus, Tito had held his portion of the southern flank and opened up the east for Stalin and Zhukov to drive them back and meet the Americans in the middle.

Vanya made a long, lazy pass over the old airbase. It had been built by the Germans, then fallen largely out of use after the war. Five years had not done much to the concrete itself, so he wondered if smugglers or spies kept it in working order these days.

Neither mattered at the moment, as he was, like Yuri had noted, a cow in a chute.

On his first pass, headlights appeared from inside a hangar

that was mostly intact to one side, though he could see where part of the roof had fallen in.

Still, someone had heard him. Noted a single jet flying low overhead.

Vanya made a second pass, but nothing caused him to worry at the moment. The space was clear. There was enough light to see by. The car had driven out to the edge of the field and parked with the lights on, just as the plan had stated.

It was now or never, though that thought passed quickly enough.

Vanya pulled back, circled a final time lowering his gear, and settled into a landing run. Risky at night, with no lights beyond the car and the moon, but the strip was a bright spot under the Hunter's Moon, and he had calibrated everything tightly for this mission before leaving Trieste, studying a number of maps, both aerial and on the ground.

Plus, he had done this a few times in training, where they had turned most of the lights off at the base in Trieste, letting the glow of the city by his guide, because Sasha believed in training and retraining.

Keeping pilots out at the edge of excellence.

Zagreb was out of sight to his right. Sound and sight and distance would hide him from them, letting those folks be snug in their beds while trouble crept about in the darkness. It would be better for most of them to never know the truth.

Vanya eased himself in slowly and delicately, keeping his Strix just above stall speed until he was over the old concrete.

Touchdown.

He let the jet roll for a distance as he slowed, then finally braked and came to rest, about midway down with that car behind him, having used their headlights to mark things for him.

Red-2 rested, then he released the brakes and fed his beast enough power to start a turn, rotating in place to get back to the car. Once there, he turned again, down at this end of the strip and facing the full length of the runway. It was more than he needed to get aloft, and he would be racing madly into that darkness when he left.

Assuming he was allowed to leave.

Now that he was on the ground, Vanya had lost all of his maneuverability. Fortunately, he had Sasha and the others aloft. If nothing else, they would be able to escape later.

Vanya assumed that his luck hung on the edge of a knife's blade. At least for now.

In place, he shut off his engines and let them whir down to silence before opening his cockpit. There was no crew in place to handle things, but he saw a pair of shapes moving around below, bringing with them a ladder that was placed against the side of his jet with a soft thump.

Vanya pulled his helmet off and rested it on the console before unbuckling and popping open the canopy. His flight suit had a space for a holster on his thigh and he touched it for luck before climbing up and then descending to the tarmac.

The night was so crisp that he could see his breath, but the suit kept him warm enough for now, and he wouldn't be on the ground all that long if things worked out correctly.

Or even if they didn't.

The two shadows resolved as Dolga's brutes, lit by his landing markers. The Croat and a second man Vanya recognized by sight, but not name.

A car door opened in the darkness and he steeled himself for what was going to come next.

Dolga emerged into the light cast by the two vehicles, with a second man trailing her. Smaller than her goons. Mousy, perhaps. A scientist, at least by stance and size compared to the two brawlers.

Vanya nodded to himself as they entered the final confrontation.

"I wasn't sure you would come," Dolga said quietly as she stepped close, the emotions in her voice muddled and unreadable.

He could see little of her, wrapped in a dark greatcoat appropriate to Moscow's winters. A long scarf hid everything but her eyes.

Just as well.

"You asked," he replied, nodding to her and the man next to her. "I came."

Vanya left it at that. The less said at this point, probably the better.

They had had their moment to resolve what had been lost a decade ago. He hoped that she would recall him with less vitriol tomorrow.

Nothing was allowed to change today.

Not even this woman that he was madly in love with.

Still, he watched the impact of his words. How they rocked her slightly back on her heels, if only for a hesitation.

Then the light went out of her eyes and she nodded to the Croat. Some message was expected, because both goons had pistols in their hands, pointed at him.

Vanya was not surprised. And had no chance to reach for his own pistol without being shot.

"It didn't have to come to this," he told her, noting that she was still unarmed.

That might matter.

And it might not.

"What is the meaning of this?" the other man demanded.

"You will still be transported to Moscow, Doctor Perko," Dolga said quietly. "However, it was necessary to use you as a lure, in order to destroy the Red Branch. They would not have come, otherwise."

Vanya shrugged, mostly with his eyes. A small enough movement to not be shot. Large enough that she could see it as they locked eyes.

I would have, he was telling her. For you.

Again, that twitch that her tradecraft could not suppress.

"What?" Perko demanded, turning to her.

The sound was dull. A thud more than a crack, though it contained elements of both. The second impact was covered by the roar of the first gunshot, sound traveling slower than bullets, even in air this cold.

Vanya ignored the two goons and had his pistol out and centered on his lover, even as both of her men were tumbled over backwards. The .375 H&H was a terrible round. A magnum load, as the Americans would have called it, designed for larger game, but adequate on something as small as a man.

"What?" Dolga asked, white as a ghost as her mind caught up.

"You really thought me that great a fool?" he asked her sharply, still ignoring Perko.

The other two were finally still on the ground, but might have died on their feet. Those bullets did terrible things. He had watched Arkadi fire enough of them at various targets, and even hunt a few deer, to worry.

"How?" she asked, brain hobbled by surprise, but Vanya presumed that she thought him a mere pilot.

A commissar.

And not the man who had trained her in tradecraft a decade ago.

He had not forgotten everything he had known.

"Put your hands up, both of you," Vanya replied, ignoring her question for now. "I am willing to finish the job, but my sniper won't kill you while you remain unarmed."

And they now could understand that he had not come alone to this place.

Arkadi had been carried in the boot of the Ambassador's car. Across the border. Into Croatia and dropped not far away yesterday.

Close enough to make this hike. To be set up at nightfall, watching.

Ready to kill a man. Or two.

Or a woman.

Lucky for Dolga that she had relied on her dead goons.

Or she would be dead now, too.

CHAPTER 53

Arkadi scanned the situation and risked his timing. The Winchester Model 70 loaded from the top, with an internal magazine. He might need to have a new version crafted by a gunsmith after this. Add a removable magazine below, because his magnum rounds only allowed three bullets internally, plus one in the barrel.

He had taken the time earlier to get a fourth in, leaving him two shots now, but Vanya had his pistol covering the two Soviet agents. Arkadi kept his eye to the scope and located the next round by touch, part of a set on a cloth wrapped around the rifle's stock.

He had done this enough times, even blindfolded, that he could retract the bolt softly, catch the round being ejected, and thumb it down into the internal magazine, following with one more, then getting his fourth in the barrel in the few seconds when the others were still paralyzed.

Arkadi had done this many times during the war. Kill one, then wait patiently for others to appear to help the target, reloading on the fly.

Normally, he had to flee after a few shots, too close to an

enemy base, where patrols could box him in. Tonight, the authorities had been told nothing, so there was no one around. Nothing but her people, two of them already dead.

Arkadi remained perfectly still as he was back to four rounds. More than enough to kill the woman and the one posing as a scientist. And nobody had been facing the right direction to even guess where he was from possibly seeing the flash of his barrel, only mostly concealed.

He settled in, zeroed on the woman's black heart and ready to kill her in an instant if she moved.

CHAPTER 54

Vanya nodded to himself as he watched Dolga do the calculations, both of the Soviet agents with their hands in the air. Like everyone else, she had only looked at the surface of the thing.

And missed the forest for all the trees.

Gennadi had created a commando unit.

Yes, they flew combat jets, but everyone had capabilities on the ground. Even the three new recruits brought with them specialist skills that filled in existing gaps, from Alfie's technical expertise to his experience with heavy weapons. Graham and *Beau* could fly, but also knew how to handle themselves with submachine guns. And would, once they were brought into the deeper conspiracy.

Perhaps never the deepest one. At least not until such a time as the Red Branch was dissolved and all of them brought home, but Vanya doubted that would be possible now.

Not after both the GRU and the MGB had lost teams to Sasha's guns.

And Vanya's.

"How?" Dolga asked, her voice no more than a whisper now.

"If I don't tell you, I won't have to kill you," he offered, mostly to watch her dark eyes grow huge in the lights of his jet.

"What is going on?" Perko demanded, still confused.

But then, they might not have told him all of the betrayals they had planned tonight.

"She hired us to transport you to Trieste in secrecy, Doctor Perko," Vanya said, glancing at the man but locked entirely on the woman.

She was far more dangerous. Arkadi was probably ready to kill her but could take out the other man quickly enough if Perko moved suddenly.

And the man understood that, because he stood perfectly still.

"However, I suspect that we'll be leaving you behind tonight," Vanya continued. "I have no interest in transporting you to Moscow, which is the promise she offered. My team and I would not be welcome there."

"You'll never escape," Dolga said sharply. "You know that, don't you?"

"No, I do not," Vanya replied.

"None of you will," she hissed, leaning into her anger finally.

Her rage. Her betrayal.

As if the Red Branch were merely a group of pilots randomly selected by Gennadi because they'd all been exiled by Moscow.

"Oh?" he prompted her, mostly to see what she thought would happen next.

"They are coming for you," Dolga nodded. "Now. Even as we speak. There are five of you. Moscow has sent fifteen MiGs to destroy you and your precious Red Branch. They will burn you to the ground."

Vanya merely smiled sadly at her.

Fool.

But then, he had also been blinded by his emotions. Fortunately, he had Sasha to rely on.

And Arkadi.

And the Red Branch.

Perko, if that was his name, moved suddenly. His hands had slowly been drooping, but Vanya had not reacted, still locked hard on Dolga Leninova.

His student. His lover.

His foe.

Perko went for a pocket.

What he thought to draw was academic, as another squishy thunk presaged the crack of a supersonic bullet impacting and tumbling the man ass over teakettle across the concrete apron.

Heavy bullet. High speed. Small target.

Death.

Vanya locked eyes with Dolga and dared her to die as well.

She finally understood. Vanya watched that moment dawn in those bottomless, dark eyes.

Arkadi would kill her without hesitation, even if Vanya didn't pull the trigger first.

And he would.

Sad, but only tomorrow.

"Well?" she demanded.

"You don't have to die," he told her. "None of this was necessary."

"You betrayed the Motherland!"

"No," Vanya replied. "I was publicly exiled as a traitor to the Soviet Union."

Even then, he had been crisp and specific with his terminology.

Dolga blinked now.

She mouthed the word *publicly?*, but no sound emerged from her mouth.

He nodded anyway, watching wheels turn within wheels in her eyes, a safe tumbler rotating to new settings. Or one of those old cryptographic machines that everyone had relied on in the war but were giving way to new electrical devices today.

"But...?"

"Not everything is as it seems, mistress," Vanya said simply. "It is all the greater sadness that nobody understands that."

"Did you betray us?" she demanded, but even then it came out no more fierce than a kitten.

"Never," he said. "However, there is nothing left for us to discuss at this point, because you have decided to kill me. And my friends."

"You can't stop it," Dolga replied, almost pleading with him now.

"And that, my love, is where you are wrong," Vanya said simply.

He drew a breath and let it go as a sigh. It might be silent, but she would see the dragon's steam. Would understand.

"Stay," she ordered softly.

"I cannot," Vanya told her. "They need me."

"What about me?" she asked as he turned away, so Vanya stopped and turned back.

"When I am in the air, you will be free to leave," he said. "I hope you can forgive me. For everything. But I must go. If I never see you again, I will still love you forever."

With that, he began jogging away, holstering his pistol and

climbing the ladder quickly, then shoving it away where it would not stop him from flying.

With one hand, he restarted the warm engines. With the other, he closed the canopy and slipped his helmet on.

"Red-1, this is Red-2," Vanya said quietly. "Launching without passenger. Repeat: without passenger."

"Red-2, this is Red-1," Sasha replied instantly. "Understood and I'm sorry. We could use your assistance up here, as all hell has broken loose."

Vanya took a moment to glance over at her, then began to throttle up his engines for take-off.

He had no doubts that the second half of her betrayal was unfolding.

CHAPTER 55

Sasha watched Vanya's jet land, nodding to himself. With any luck, things would unfold differently than the mission he had laid out, but Sasha knew no doubts.

Dolga Leninova, the *Dutiful Daughter Of Lenin*, would not betray Moscow. Not even when her rage met her uncertainty at killing the man Sasha thought she might still love.

But it didn't matter. Not now. Not tonight.

"Red-4 and Red-6, you will form up and begin your assigned patrol," he ordered. "Standard pattern, low enough to be seen from the ground."

"Roger that, Red-1," *Beau* replied, the more senior of the two based solely on having been hired two weeks earlier.

Both men were twenty-five, making him feel practically ancient at thirty-six, but both were experts with a lot of experience and sound judgment.

Temperament had been one of the first filters Gennadi had applied, washing out the hotshots and troublemakers even before sending any names on to Sasha for review, because a mercenary company had no space for that sort of person, regardless of their skill.

Sasha squared his shoulders once.

"Red-3, move to Rendezvous Position One," Sasha continued. "Red-1 moving to Rendezvous Position Two."

"Understood, *Cernunnos*," *Banshee* replied. "Executing now."

In a perfect world, she would simply move to that spot, linger for a time, and then return.

Sasha didn't believe it for a moment.

"Red-5, you have command," Sasha ordered.

"Red-5, taking command," Dmitri replied instantly. "All skies clear to the limits of radar."

As was to be expected.

For now.

Vanya would need time on the ground, whatever was to happen. Or how it would unfold.

He turned and moved to the northwest of Zagreb, picking out a spot he knew from previous night patrols.

"Alfie, anything interesting?" he asked on the inside line.

"Negative, Commander," his backseat sidekick replied immediately. "We expecting trouble this quickly?"

"We are not," Sasha said. "But shortly."

"Roger that, sir."

Sasha let the night embrace him.

Yuri still wanted a gunship. Something big and fast and silly and heavily armed, like an American B-50, the upgraded B-29, only with heavier guns and jet engines on the wings that let him keep up with Sasha and the others.

He also wanted a unicorn, for what it was worth.

The Camel, his heavily camouflaged Il-28 Medium Bomber, had a ceiling of 13,700 meters. Higher than most, but he understood that the MiG-15 could reach 15,500, so they might be lurking above him, save that those aircraft were dangerous to fly as one approached Mach-flight. Unstable.

Better to simply go fast, while staying high enough.

Yuri presumed that trouble would come in lower, where they might hope to catch Vanya on the ground. And surprise everyone else.

Thus, instead of a normal orbital pattern, tonight he was flying a series of swoops from northwest to southeast and back, drawing the Camel's nose across the east and northeast regularly, where he expected trouble.

Sasha had simply marked a series of air bases across the Romanian border without getting any more specific, but Yuri had flown with the man the longest. Probably knew him the best.

"Dmitri, have you found them yet?" he asked simply.

"Negative, Yuri," Dmitri answered from the nose, with his radars and bombsights. "But I doubt that it will long coming."

"Oleg, are you awake back there?" Yuri asked.

"Anything is possible, Yuri," Oleg replied with a chuckle.

As if any of them could sleep, knowing tonight's mission.

"Yuri, I have a possible contact," Oleg suddenly announced. "Russian voices talking on a channel normally assigned to Soviet Air Forces. Everything is cryptic but sounds military and prepared."

In addition to controlling the rear-facing turret, Oleg's station handled the long-range radio, though they hardly ever used such a thing, the Red Branch talking within the squadron on a different frequency.

Still, they were prepared.

"I have them," Dmitri announced. "Zero-seven-zero and approaching. A cluster of aircraft moving at jet speeds. Repeat, enemy jet squadron closing at high speed. All Red Branch aircraft stand by for combat operations."

"Red-5, this is Red-1," Sasha replied. "Taking command. *Banshee*, initiate your operations and stand by to engage."

Yuri looked at what was coming and decided that he did not need to be in the middle of it. Not a dogfight in moonlight over Yugoslavia.

"Red-team, this is Red-5," he called. "Moving to Rendezvous Point Seven for observation. Repeat, Rendezvous Point Seven."

Safely off to the northwest, where his radar could still cover things and keep any more surprises from slipping and threatening, without himself being all that exposed.

The Camel did bite. Two forward cannons in the nose plus two more aft with Oleg on the controls. And the aircraft was nimble enough to slip away from someone trying to catch him broadside.

At least in Yuri's hands.

But he had no business in this mess.

At least until that American woman built him a unicorn.

CHAPTER 57

Sasha felt bad that his first response was simply an acknowledgment that he'd been right.

That trouble had come looking for them.

That Leninova had betrayed Vanya, down there on the ground.

Hopefully, Arkadi was the surprise Vanya needed to balance those scales of justice.

Or tip them.

But that would be resolved another time.

"Red-team, this is Red-5," Dmitri announced. "Incoming enemy force estimated at fifteen aircraft. Speed and vector suggest MiG-15s on intercept course. Time to contact three minutes."

Sasha nodded again. Almost exactly on time, when he'd been guessing based entirely on the ground schedule Leninova had laid out.

"Red-1, this is Red-2," Vanya was suddenly there on the radio. "Launching without passenger. Repeat: without passenger."

"Red-2, this is Red-1," Sasha answered. "Understood and

I'm sorry. We could use your assistance up here, as all hell has broken loose."

"I will be along as quickly as I can," Vanya replied.

Sasha knew that. And heard the sadness in his friend's voice. They would probably have to get the man excessively drunk later, though Sasha had no idea if Vanya was a happy drunk or a maudlin one.

Always a man under perfect control of himself, which was why he had been promoted to commissar. And why Gennadi had asked him to join the Red Branch.

For now, it was what it was. Sasha switched radio channels.

"Blue squadron, this is Red-1," he said, calling into the darkness as he checked that fuel was at good levels and all his cannons were armed and ready. "What is your status?"

"Red-1, this is Blue Leader," a man's voice answered instantly. "We are in position and standing by for your orders, sir."

Sasha ground his teeth once. Crushed nothingness between them that it had come to this. That his mission had failed.

At the same time, it was obvious that the Soviet Union never intended to let him succeed, despite all public assurances of neutrality. But then, who was neutral here?

Sasha had sent a message to General Stoddard. Had signaled that this was probably the emergency that they had planned against before he ever left California.

Stoddard had been right then. And he was right now.

"Blue squadron, you maintain formation and I will come over the top of you will all my lights on and lead you in," Sasha said. "Enemy jets are approaching at high speed from the northeast, but they will have no better night visibility than you do, because Red Force has the only night-fighters aloft tonight."

"Roger that, Red-1," Blue Leader replied.

"Alfie, you have them?" Sasha asked.

"Come right twenty degrees and climb a shade, Commander," Alfie said. "We'll reverse back in thirty seconds and then insert."

"Excellent work, Alfie," Sasha said.

He'd worried about putting the newest man here, but Alfie Hirano had a lifetime of fitting into foreign cultures. Then rising to his excellence with every one of them. He could handle this.

It might be interesting, the first time they hired a pilot who had not seen combat in the Great Patriotic War, but Alfie had served with the American 442nd Regimental Combat Team, entirely composed of Japanese-American soldiers and assigned the hardest tasks in Europe.

And the most decorated American unit in the war.

The next war had arrived tonight. Sasha had to make sure it didn't get out of hand, even as he made it a point to shove someone back across that line that was usually draped by an Iron Curtain.

Tito's people had demanded that the Red Branch protect them, at least for a time.

He had a job to do.

CHAPTER 58

Lyuba could see the dots of the other aircraft in the distance. Yanina had been quietly calling out range and heading as both groups circled.

She switched radio channels and opened her circle wider.

"Gold Squadron, this is Red-3," she said. "Callsign *Banshee*. Approaching your position shortly. Stand by to form up on my aircraft and engage enemy squadron."

There was a pause she was entirely expecting. American pilots.

Even the good ones had a strong strain of sexism in them that most could not overcome. Even after he'd been warned that she was coming.

"*Banshee*, this is Gold Leader," a man replied with a hesitation in his voice like a seed struck in his teeth. "Confirming operational readiness."

She reached down and brought all her exterior lights on, the better for those men to see her.

It would have been nice to have some of the men from Edwards, but those were the test pilots, while these men were the combat fliers over Europe, prepared to resist a Soviet invasion.

"Gold Leader, I have over seven thousand hours in the air," she said simply. "And I used to bomb Nazi formations from lower than two hundred meters with the engines on my biplane turned off so we could sneak up on them silently. We'll be blasting through the enemy formation at high speed, firing as you go. Form up on my aircraft and stand by to dive."

Mostly, *Banshee* kept the acid-dipped razors out of her voice. She could always yell at them later.

Or pass a message along to General Stoddard and let him issue disciplinary rebukes. None of these men had ever dealt with a woman combat pilot, obviously.

"Did you say seven *thousand* hours," a different man asked, disbelief evident in his voice.

"I was with the 46th Guards Night Bomber Aviation Regiment," *Banshee* growled at those *boys*. "The Nazis called us the *Night Witches* when we came for them. I flew strike missions six days per week for over four years."

Silence. Probably aghast. She might have more flight hours than all of these men put together, as little time as they normally spent in the air these days.

Banshee assumed that she had also killed more people than most of the pilots she would ever meet.

"*Banshee*, this is Gold Leader, we're ready for you to lead us in."

"Excellent," *Banshee* replied. "Stand by to come left and engage."

CHAPTER 59

Banshee listened as Yanina and Dmitri conferred on a different channel.

Fifteen MiGs. Closing at high speed and preparing to jump *Beau*, *Devonshire*, and *Ecne* when he got aloft.

We will see about that.

She glanced back both ways at Gold Squadron, a team of the new F-86 Sabrejets, like she had flown in and against at Edwards. Day fighters, so not equipped with radar or a spotter. Lightly armed by her standards, flying with 12.7mm machine guns. The American M3 Browning. Six of them them per aircraft, but the MiGs were better armored, which was why she had insisted that Kelly put 30mm ADEN revolvers in the Strix.

Still, her job tonight was to inject chaos. With a little help from her friends.

"Gold Squadron, this is *Banshee*," *Banshee* announced. "Diving now."

She pushed her joystick forward and accelerated without bothering to see if those men were joining her.

Or keeping up.

She had a job to do. And Sasha needed her breaking up the enemy formation before he pounced on them next.

"Yanina?" she asked on the intercom.

"None of those boys wish to be shown up by a mere woman," Yanina answered from the back seat, chuckling.

Banshee matched her. Of course not. They all saw themselves as big, bad American fighter pilots.

She had just spent much of a year flying with the men at Muroc/Edwards. The test pilots who were the cream of the American crop.

And holding her own.

"Gold Squadron, this is Red-Base," Dmitri announced on the line. "Enemy force has not, repeat NOT, detected you inbound."

Banshee smiled.

Nobody else had jet night-fighters yet, though she assumed that everyone would be building them soon, such as the Lockheed F-94 that Kelly had gotten this cockpit from to adapt his XF-90 into the F-90B.

Certainly, the MiG-15 was not ready for her.

"Gold Squadron, this is Red-Base," Dmitri followed up ten seconds later. "You have been detected by the enemy force. Stand by to engage."

"Gold Squadron, increase acceleration," *Banshee* ordered.

They were already closing at impossible speeds, coming from the right of the MiGs and slightly above, about to dive through their formation like hawks.

Because Vanya had assumed his lover would betray them and told Sasha to ask for help.

Two squadrons of American Sabres assisted the Red Branch tonight.

Not entirely fair, but *Banshee* had no doubts that someone

would eventually build a night-fighter that could engage the Strix on even terms.

That was not tonight, though.

Banshee located the flight leader of the MiGs as she closed, aware of how those pilots were trained. Even good ones from Soviet squadrons instead of lesser pilots in lesser aircraft.

She centered her targeting circle and led the man, then opened up as she got close, hawks and pigeons suddenly turning every which way.

"Gold Squadron, stay on *Banshee*," Yanina barked sharply into the radio, even as *Banshee* swept through the MiG formation. "Maintain formation for the next pass."

No doubt, some of those boys would be overly excited and turn to duel. To dogfight.

In the darkness of a full moon, there was just enough light to do it.

And the MiG-15 looked too much like an F-86 at high speeds to know for certain who you were shooting at, once formations broke apart. She would kill anybody flying alone.

Then she was through, like a bullet passing through a body.

"Gold Squadron, maintain formation and prepare to come right and climb in ten seconds," *Banshee* ordered. "We'll draw them in and then get another pass at them."

"You heard the lady," Gold Leader barked when some of his men began to complain. "Follow orders."

Because someone, somewhere, had made sure that that man understood the stakes tonight.

CHAPTER 60

Vanya climbed, leaving Dolga behind to whatever fate she chose for herself.

Hopefully, it would be a good one. One where they could remember what they had had, and lost, and found again.

And now lost again.

But it had been worth it.

"Red-4, what is our status?" Vanya asked as he got aloft.

Without Arkadi behind him, he was as blind as the fools launching an attack in day-fighters.

Against a radar-equipped enemy.

There were less painful ways to commit suicide, but the Soviet Union hadn't asked him. Had merely ordered those men out to die.

"We have you on our radar," *Beau* replied. "Maintain course and climb and we'll form on your wings in thirty seconds. *Banshee* has intercepted the enemy squadron and is currently leading them off."

"Remember that I'm blind here," Vanya said.

"Affirmative," *Beau* replied. "Commander wants you in the middle where we're keeping you safe."

Vanya swallowed past a throat too tight, appreciating that he had friends tonight. People worried about him and looking out.

Understanding that his final confrontation with Dolga might have left him too unsettled to make good decisions.

He rose, noting various lights as many aircraft jostled for position above them.

"We're still running for a corner and then climbing up and over to swoop back in?" *Devonshire* asked.

"Affirmative," *Beau* replied. "We've got radar and they don't, as long as they stay in teams we can identify."

"Red-2, this is Red-Base," Dmitri said. "Stand by as a blocking force that will move due north, then be ready to intercept and engage enemy aircraft breaking away to run for home."

"Roger that, Red-Base," Vanya answered. "We'll move into position now."

It was a mess, but Sasha had looked at everything and read Dolga's heart and soul as well as Vanya had.

For all the good it had done him.

CHAPTER 61

Sasha looked back in both directions, down his wings at two lines of Sabres trailing below him and back like geese. And they were headed south.

"Alfie, call the mark," he said simply, the switched from intercom to Blue frequency.

"Blue Squadron, stand by," Alfie replied quietly. "I want them a little more broken up first. Looks like *Banshee* might have scored a kill on her pass. Others are hurting, but only one is breaking down too fast and alone. The remainder appear to be turning to chase *Banshee*. Okay, there. Red-Base, do you confirm?"

"Roger that, Red-1," Dmitri replied.

"Blue Squadron, this is Red-1, dive and engage. Do not dogfight your targets, as only Red Branch aircraft are easily identifiable at night. Hit them and keep going, then form up and we'll circle back for another bite."

Because that was what this was. Sharks, pouncing on seals form multiple directions. Orcas and tuna.

After tonight, Sasha had no doubts that the Soviet Union

would look much closer at what he had built and design an operation capable of taking them on directly.

How their spies had missed what Kelly and Woodie had done for them beggared the imagination, but he wasn't about to look a gift horse in the mouth.

Below, the MiGs had turned to chase *Banshee*.

As intended.

And one of them was on fire, a meteor falling out of the sky while the others raced after Gold Squadron.

"Blue Squadron, throttle back," Sasha ordered. "Engage from high aft but do not fly through their formation. We will dive and roll away to our right shortly."

"Roger that, Red Leader," Blue Leader replied. "Engaging now."

Tracer bullets erupted all around him, phosphorescent hoses of fire reaching out to touch the MiGs so thick you might think a dragon was breathing fire.

Only 12.7mm, though. .50 caliber bullets, which had been outdated even before the end of the Great Patriotic War as designers added armor and toughened up their aircraft to resist.

The Americans should have upgraded at least to the 20mm cannon, like the Soviet Union had done in the MiGs, as well as in the now-retired Nightvipers that had been grounded for the F-90B Strix.

Still, one had to be careful because the MiG-15 also had a 37mm Nudelman N-37 autocannon, capable of doing great damage, save that it and the 20mm cannons were not aimed at the same points forward.

Sasha's MiG caught fire, a wing shedding parts before the pilot understood that they were suddenly surrounded again.

Someone awoke and began issuing orders over there, because the Soviet pilots all began to dive.

"Blue Squadron, this is Red Leader," Sasha ordered. "All aircraft pull up and let the Soviets escape for now. I want us out of the way when Gold Squadron makes their second pass. Red-Base, call the operation."

"Blue force is moving out of the engagement zone," Dmitri replied. "Gold force, stand by to attack. Enemy squadron has broken into two main pieces and has not yet begun to regroup. *Banshee*, you will engage the force on your left as you close, with numerical superiority. Blue force, stand by to come hard about and engage the force that will be on your right after a reverse. Maintain formation and you will outnumber them two to one in both groups. Engage and destroy."

Sasha wanted to stand his aircraft on one wing and snap right back over, but his American pilots were not as well trained for night flying in formation and would risk touching wingtips catastrophically if they got too ambitious.

Instead, he rode it forward some.

"Blue force, any problems with returning to engage?" he asked.

"Negative, Red Leader," Blue Leader replied. "Standing by to turn."

"Blue force, come left on my count and accelerate after we complete our circle," Sasha ordered. "Begin your turn now."

Someone had sent an entire squadron of MiGs to kill him tonight, expecting to have at least triple his number of aircraft to offset Sasha's radar.

They had not bothered watching American bases in Italy sending Sabres aloft at night, which should have been a clue that something was desperately wrong somewhere.

And these had to be Soviet pilots, as the Romanians didn't have jets in their inventory yet, though he could see that changing soon.

Piston-driven aircraft had no business in combat with jets, night or day.

Not in a feeding frenzy like this.

CHAPTER 62

Banshee led her team in, drifting everyone back on their throttles and coming up from below and the left. She raked the central jet with cannon fire and got a lucky hit, because the aircraft detonated instead of catching fire.

A fireball that lit up the entire night in every direction and probably frightened civilians in Zagreb. But at least they could say definitively that the Red Branch was protecting Yugoslav airspace.

The remaining five aircraft dove, but that walked them across the guns of the Sabres around here, and two more started trailing flames that made them even better targets.

"Gold Team, slow down and turn to engage," she ordered. "Blue Team has the other group."

The MiGs could outclimb the Sabres, but didn't have the ability to outrun them. Nor her.

Especially not with Yuri sitting off on one corner of the battlefield, watching everything and able to call things.

The MiGs realized that and began to climb. That was their only chance, as the MiG-15 could get higher than the F-86.

But not the F-90B Strix. She would deal with them alone if

she had to, but they had already been spooked and damaged to the point that the Red Branch might take them in a straight up dogfight.

"Gold Squadron, this is Red-Base. Break off immediately. Repeat, break off pursuit."

"Understood, Red-Base," *Banshee* replied. "Breaking off. Gold Team, drop elevation and orbit left **now**."

"They only think they are getting away," Yanina said quietly. "Someone forgot about Vanya and the other two.

Banshee smiled. There was a reason she'd gone after their commander up front. None of the Russian pilots were ever trained or prepared to immediately step in and replace someone like that, making them that much more fragile in battle.

She looked around and noted that the Sabres were doing a good job of keeping up with her, even as several shooting stars below looked to be slamming into the ground soon.

"Parachutes?" she asked.

"About half," Yanina replied. "I presume *Cernunnos* will inform the Yugoslav authorities and someone will activate their Partisans to hunt those men."

More chuckles. Some of the most dangerous soldiers in the entire war had been those Partisans. Almost as nasty, kilo for kilo, as Finns. The Soviet pilots would hopefully only be captured and arrested, so they could be traded home, as Yugoslavia wasn't at war with Russia.

Merely arguing like siblings.

For now.

Tomorrow might bring a whole different raft of difficulties.

CHAPTER 63

Vanya listened in as Dmitri lined them up. There was a certain cruelty to it, like a farmer culling his sheep for winter.

At the same time, they had started it. Had come for him, when he had been willing to answer Dolga's call for help.

It had all been a sham, but as Yuri had noted, they were cattle in a chute after a certain point. Actors with a script they could only follow. Hamlet, perhaps. Or those two fools Rosencrantz and Guildenstern, sent to their deaths for trusting that they had outsmarted their old friend, only to be killed on arrival.

Tonight, he would have to take a lesson from Horatio, the only survivor of that day.

It was necessary to survive.

"Red-2, this is Red-4, stand by to drift back on my wing in a sliding formation," *Beau* called quietly.

Sasha watched that aircraft come forward, then settled, with *Devonshire* back on his left.

"Red-4, this is Red-Base, you are clear to engage group two," Dmitri called.

"Tally ho," *Beau* replied. "*Ecne*, here we go."

Vanya nodded and drew a breath. Bygones would be recriminations to meditate upon tomorrow, after he had gotten home safely. For now, he had a job to do, as *Beau* nosed over and started to accelerate.

Vanya picked them up. Three silver darts turned and racing madly from right to left, noses turned northwest and engines wide open like rockets lighting the night.

He supposed that it might be a pity that the MiG-15, while incredibly maneuverable, could not outrun the Strix. Only outclimb, but they had to get there first and were currently flying level to get the greatest distance possible.

"Engaging now," *Beau* called. "Split and take them as you bear. Red-2, rely on Red-Base to be your eyes."

Vanya had worried about hiring the Australian bush pilot with the immense personality. The man had only been a Flight Sergeant during the war, those forces not automatically commissioning a pilot as an officer. The Japanese had been the same way.

All doubts had long since evaporated and *Beau* brought them around, accelerating after the three MiGs. Vanya watched the rear pilot jolt as he saw three owls come hunting, wings waggling slightly.

"There they go," *Devonshire* called. "I have the leader."

"Tail Gun Charlie's mine," *Beau* answered.

That left the one in the middle for Vanya. That pilot did himself no good by dithering for a long second as the other two split away, every man seemingly for himself at this moment.

The MiG-15 was agile. The Strix durable. He could hold more torque than the Russian plane, as that pilot started a dive.

And Vanya could easily blow past Mach One, while the MiG began to wobble badly as it crossed Mach 0.9.

Vanya had to throttle back and time his shot as the Russian

pilot flared and jinked, unable to escape and perhaps unaware that he could get away if he climbed.

Of course, that would slow him tremendously.

There.

Vanya triggered his cannons and let light connect the two aircraft for a long moment.

The MiG was a durable aircraft, but the 30mm ADEN was heavier than the Soviet designers had anticipated. The British had already announced that all new aircraft would have such guns in the future, while the Americans dithered between the underpowered 12.7mm machine gun and the silliness of rocket packs randomly flying and hoping for a blind kill.

The ADEN was an executioner's ax.

The MiG flew directly into a burst, but for a moment Vanya wondered if he had mistimed his shot.

Until the MiG shattered, followed an instant later by an explosion that lit the night sky and forced Vanya to roll onto a wing and pull up to avoid debris.

Looking around, two other flaming comets were already falling from the night sky.

"Red Branch, this is Red-Base," Dmitri called. "MiG Force One is destroyed. Blue Squadron, stand by to destroy MiG Force Two. Gold Squadron, come left, elevate, and stand by to herd any strays. Red-2, turn to zero-nine-zero and maintain elevation so you can block off anyone trying to run. Wait. Stand by. All Red Branch elements, this is Red-Base. MiG Force Two has surrendered. Repeat, surrendered. Red-1, take command."

Vanya nodded.

Sasha could deal with them.

Vanya needed time to mourn.

CHAPTER 64

Sasha glanced right and left, confirming the Sabres that had done such an excellent job as a strike force tonight, when he'd been worried about them shattering into individual duels that lost all the benefit of numbers and radar.

"Alfie, I need their channel," he said.

"Stand by, Commander," Alfie replied. "Now."

"This is *Cernunnos*, Commander of the Red Branch," Sasha announced in hard, angry Russian. "Surviving MiG pilots, you will come to two-one-five and direct your course to a base west of Zagreb. Any deviation from that flight path and you will be destroyed without a second warning. Begin reducing your flight elevation to four thousand meters and maintain there until you have the base in sight, wherein you will immediately land and surrender. Those are your terms. Am I clear?"

"This is Romanian Flight Seventeen," a man replied. "We hear and obey, Red Branch. Initiating now."

Three MiGs, out of fifteen. Against five radar-equipped Strix and the Camel, plus two squadrons of F-86 Sabres.

Not even remotely fair, but Sasha had had to assume that

Leninova was baiting a trap. That the MGB thought they could crush or capture the Red Branch tonight with the right bait.

And she probably had been.

Might yet be, but her cover was likely entirely blown at this point.

What happened to her tomorrow wasn't his problem.

Sasha switched channels back and spoke in English.

"Red Branch Force, this is Red-1," he said sternly. "Enemy fighters are following orders to land at Zagreb. Red-Base, your task is to make sure nobody else tries my patience tonight."

"All clear on all approaches, Commander," Dmitri replied in a subdued voice that let Sasha know how angry he sounded.

The Americans merely flew, maintaining tight formations and professional skill, like this might be an audition.

It wasn't, but he didn't bother telling them that. Back in California, Gennadi had a second stack of resumes he was studying, including several American pilots that Lockwood Carlyle had suggested.

Tomorrow's task. Tonight, he had other problems to solve as he changed radio frequencies again.

"Zagreb Control, this *Cernunnos* of the Red Branch," he called. "Reply on this frequency."

"Red Branch, this is Zagreb Control," Ambassador Ćosić was there immediately. "We have been following your operation. Stand by for runway lights to come fully active. We are clearing the tarmac and sounding the alert."

"As long as you do not launch any aircraft, Zagreb," Sasha replied. "I want these three safely landed and under your control so you can trade them home later. Additionally, there will be twelve other pilots to account for, but I cannot tell you how many will make it successfully to the ground. That is the nature of night combat."

"Understood, Red Branch," Ćosić said. "We are activating patrol forces and will be initiating roadblocks and sweeps."

"Thank you, Zagreb Control," Sasha said. "We will return to base once your portion of the mission is complete. We will await updates and orders from there."

Sasha didn't say it over an open line but presumed that Tito would immediately fire them for dealing with Soviet secret agents and attempting to smuggle a scientist out of Yugoslavia, even as it had been part of the cover that would let the man uncover all of Leninova's friends.

The American and British authorities in the Free City would begin arresting people by morning, based on information that Sasha had conveyed to General Stoddard, in his role as part of US Air Force Intelligence. And that man's connections to the new Central Intelligence Agency the Americans had created to resist the efforts of the MGB.

Tomorrow threatened to be just as stressful as tonight, but at least it was likely coming to some sort of conclusion.

Wherever this road took them.

CHAPTER 65

Vanya watched the three MiGs come to a stop surrounded by tanks and jeeps with machine-guns, so those men would be taken into custody. Tito did not desire an open war with Stalin, so presumably they would be safely home, though their fate there might be bad enough to induce them to defect to Yugoslavia instead.

Or Trieste. The Free City wasn't that far away, at least physically.

"Gold Squadron, this is *Banshee*," she called. "Thank you for your assistance tonight. You may return to base."

"Excellent, Madame Night Witch," a man replied. "Do not hesitate to contact us next time you need a strike force."

On his left, Vanya watched that block of aircraft turn as one and head off into the night.

"Blue Squadron, this is Red-1, you are cleared to return home and thank you."

"Thank you, Red Branch," a man replied. "Be seeing you around."

And the other half split, leaving only five F-90B Strix

escorting one Camel as they turned southwest and started the glide into Trieste, suddenly alone in the night sky.

Across that magical line that meant the Red Branch was in international territory, rather than behind the Iron Curtain, however thin and gauzy it might be in this corner of Croatia.

It was still a line separating east from west. Him from Dolga.

Yesterday from tomorrow.

And tomorrow, he would be going home.

CHAPTER 66
CHAPTER

Vanya woke to a rap at his closed door, having slept in far longer today. Yesterday, they had napped some while briefing various generals and politicians on everything that had happened, including the failed defection of Perko, who had turned out to be yet another MGB secret agent in Vanya's semi-lurid retelling of things.

If it was necessary to slander the dead, the man had brought it upon himself.

Vanya stirred and sat up, having fallen on his bed last night in uniform pants and T-shirt, too tired to do more than strip his tunic and his boots before collapsing.

The woodpecker at his door insisted.

"Coming," he answered, loud enough to make them stop.

At least for now.

Vanya found his tunic and belted it into place, stuffing feet into boots and ignoring the holster for now.

No alarms had been sounded, so it couldn't be more than a mild catastrophe at this point.

He opened the door to find Arkadi standing there, smiling wryly.

Vanya had never been a tactile person, but he engulfed the smaller man in a tremendous hug that tried to convey everything, because this man had been his guardian angel on all those nights.

Including the one that mattered.

"I have news," Arkadi said as they stepped back and grinned at one another.

"Oh?" Vanya asked.

"Come," Arkadi waved, starting to walk away. "You will need coffee and perhaps a pastry as you digest it all."

Vanya's stomach rumbled in agreement and he fell into the man's wake, headed towards the kitchen and wardroom.

He stopped at the door, breath exploding out of his chest as though someone had punched him in the stomach and gasping.

Dolga sat at a table with a concerned look on her face, bracketed by Lyuba and Sasha.

Vanya could not will his feet to cross that threshold, until Arkadi grabbed him by an arm and dragged him to the table, practically forcing him to sit across from the woman.

Nobody else in the room except the Red Branch, which today included the three newest members: Alfie, *Devonshire*, and *Beau*.

Vanya blinked several times, uncertain if he yet dreamed.

And if it was a nightmare or his fondest haunting him.

"How?" he finally managed.

"Arkadi chose not to kill me," Dolga explained quietly, nodding to the sniper who was even then returning with two mugs of coffee.

Vanya found a plate of rolls at hand and stuffed one into his mouth, both to buy time and to get it to close when it wished to simply hang open forever.

A sip of coffee barely served to warm him from the ball of ice that had formed in his belly.

And Arkadi had chosen not to kill her?

Vanya turned to his partner and Arkadi simply nodded sagely. But then, the man had seen himself as Zeus atop Olympus with his mighty thunderbolts. Had he not so described things?

Vanya turned to Sasha next, because obviously he had missed something important here.

How long had they let him sleep in? Long enough that Sasha nodded as well, so *Cernunnos* had gotten whatever story Dolga had to share.

And approved.

"We have been recalled," Sasha said simply. "Officially ordered to withdraw and not return, though Ambassador Ćosić conveyed quiet thanks for handling this mission as we did. The Red Branch mission to the Free City ends at noon today."

As he had expected. Vanya had heard Sasha lay out the most likely timeline, assuming that his own triple-cross of Dolga's double- would play out a certain way.

Apparently, it had.

Vanya turned back to Dolga and watched her, even as he spoke to Sasha.

"What happens next, Commander?" he asked quietly, aware that the entire Red Branch was within the sound of his voice, including Arkadi who had had to vanish into the woods to make all this possible.

Again.

"We will stand down our patrols," Sasha replied. "Everyone has completed maintenance on their aircraft, so we are prepared to lift off later today and return as far as Ireland for refueling and making the run to Washington, D.C. and points beyond tomorrow."

It was the *points beyond* that had Vanya's attention. The Americans would not appreciate nor approve an MGB agent like her in their country, yet he could think of no other reason for Dolga Leninova to be seated across from him, almost timid amidst this group.

But then, the Red Branch hadn't just defeated her trap. Sasha had annihilated it.

How would Moscow treat her afterwards? Probably the same Siberian camp the rest of them might face.

Those of them that weren't going to simply be shot out of hand.

"Just like that?" he asked Sasha, turning to look at the man.

"Ambassador Ćosić delivered the two of them to our gate in his own vehicle, along with Tito's official dismissal," Sasha said, leaving out all the rest of the details.

At least for now.

Vanya concentrated on Dolga.

"I will be branded a failure," she said. "Presumably a turn-coat, for how badly the Red Branch out-maneuvered me and my forces. I could return home, possibly vanish into the bowels of the Lubyanka forever, or I could disappear now."

The Lubyanka. The single most vile prison in the Soviet Union, possibly in the world, where Beria and his predecessors had people taken to be interrogated.

And vanished.

Or she could defect, as she presumed that he had done. That they had all done, because even an agent as good as Dolga Leninova had not been able to pierce the veil of secrecy that surrounded the Red Branch.

But Gennadi had been playing games with death as the

most likely outcome, so he had sought long and far for the men and women who could best surmount those odds.

The Red Branch.

"You can never go home," he told her simply.

"I can never go home now, Vanya," she replied, eyes ancient beyond her years. "If you would have me."

If? Vanya could think of no outcome he desired more in this world, but it was not his decision.

Not today.

He turned to Sasha.

Cernunnos.

Red-1.

"She and I have spoken," Sasha said diplomatically. "Arkadi spoke up for her, after rescuing her from Zagreb."

Rescuing?

He turned to Arkadi. The grin was back, like this was all a terrible practical joke on someone.

And it was, in its own way.

"What will the Generals think?" Vanya asked, as it appeared that the others had already reached some conclusion.

"I will speak with them," Sasha said. "They will listen, or we will return to South America or wherever else our next contract takes us."

The impact of those words stole all his air again. Sasha would lock horns with the American government itself over this woman spy who had tried to kill all of them?

But then, even at the end she had implored him to stay on the ground, when she knew that the others were doomed.

That he might survive. That they might know something of love in whatever tomorrow was coming.

Even as things had turned out differently.

And Arkadi had chosen not to kill her.

Vanya had no words. None.

All of his life he had been a loner by choice. The cold, calm, logical, rational creature that the other spies had steered clear of. That the pilots had been unable to understand, but had to accept because he could outfly them.

It felt strange to *belong*.

And yet, he did, surrounded by the Red Branch, which had somehow morphed into a new family for all of them.

And he might have Dolga, as well.

He held out a hand timidly, afraid.

She grasped it like a drowning woman and crushed his fingers holding on, so Vanya felt better.

A woman like Dolga could be frightened of all this, too.

But then, she had somehow convinced Arkadi. Had gotten him to speak for her. To carry her in the Yugoslav ambassador's car to their gate, when they were more likely to shoot her as a Soviet spy.

Had convinced Sasha and Lyuba.

He turned to *Banshee*. Watched her eyes, because she was a woman and would see and know things that Vanya would miss.

Especially when he might be a little blinded.

"I am convinced," Lyuba pronounced.

That was sufficient. Lyuba was one of the smartest people he knew. And among the most dangerous, even in this room.

Vanya turned to Sasha.

"How do we manage it?" he asked, since everything else seemed a done deal.

But how did they get a Soviet spy out of Trieste and to America, when her own people were no doubt hunting her.

Or would be, soon.

"Arkadi will fly commercial," Sasha grinned. "She will ride with you."

Fitting, Vanya supposed.

He turned to Arkadi. The grin was a broad smile and a nod.

They could get Dolga to Washington, where no doubt Sasha would radio ahead from Ireland and ask General Carlyle to meet them. And possibly General Stoddard.

And whoever else could keep a secret.

But they were the Red Branch, and could keep the deepest secrets imaginable.

At some point, Vanya knew there would be a reckoning over all the lies and deceptions, but until then, he could have his stolen moments with Dolga.

A thought jarred him.

"You cannot remain Dolga Leninova," Vanya reminded her. "Not if all this succeeds."

Sasha had a sour look on his face, as did Lyuba, as neither of them had made that connection.

"Would an American be able to distinguish Siberian from Japanese?" Nikon asked abruptly.

Every head turned to the man, another quiet one along the edges who understood his role and his place but was willing to speak up when the situation demanded it.

That was why the Red Branch worked so well, when a unit of Soviet drones would have long-since failed.

Sasha wanted your mind and your expertise.

"Unlikely," Vanya replied, a sudden smile warming his face. "It is unfortunate, but true that there is a tendency to lump all Asians into a single ethnic group without any finer gradations."

Nikon nodded, then turned to Alfie Hirano.

"I remember a woman during the war," Nikon said. "A Japanese comrade who helped deliver arms and equipment.

Her name was Takako. Alfie, does it mean what I think I remember?"

Heads turned again, this time to the newest team member, who was Japanese-American, but had been American for many generations.

Alfie's face screwed up tight, eyes squinted.

"Taka and ko," he mused. "The former conveys duty and respect. The latter is the Japanese ending for child. Organized like that, Dutiful Child, more or less. Honorable Daughter, maybe."

"Perfect," Nikon beamed. "I have no idea what an appropriate surname equivalent might be, but it is a start."

Dolga turned to him with wariness and surprise. Vanya held her hand and smiled.

"Indeed," he told her. Told all of them. "It is a start."

ABOUT THE AUTHOR

Blaze Ward writes science fiction in the Alexandria Station universe (Jessica Keller, The Science Officer, First Centurion Kosnett, etc.) as well as The Corsac Fox and several other science fiction universes. He also writes action-thriller (present day as well as historic). In addition, he's the editor and publisher of Boundary Shock Quarterly Magazine and Thrill Ride Magazine. You can find out more at his website www.blazeward.com, as well as Bluesky, Goodreads, and other places.

Blaze's works are available as ebooks, paper, and audio, and can be found at a variety of online vendors (Kobo, Amazon, and others) as well as the Knotted Road Press website directly. His newsletter comes out monthly and you can also follow his blog and his Patreon on his website. He really enjoys interacting with fans, and looks forward to any and all questions—even ones about his books!

Never miss a release!
If you'd like to be notified of new releases, sign up for my newsletter.

http://www.blazeward.com/newsletter/

Buy More!

Did you know that you can buy directly from the KRP website?

https://www.knottedroadpress.com/shop/

Connect with Blaze!

Web: www.blazeward.com
Boundary Shock Quarterly (BSQ):
https://www.boundaryshockquarterly.com/

ABOUT KNOTTED ROAD PRESS

Knotted Road Press publishes dynamic fiction set in exotic locations. Our authors cover a wide range of genres including science fiction, fantasy, mystery, literary, and poetry. We also have unique non-fiction voices in genres such as autobiography, business, cookbooks, and how-tos. We offer both DRM-free ebooks and print books for a global readership.

www.KnottedRoadPress.com